A GEORGIANA GERMAINE MYSTERY

LITTLE WHITE LIES

CHERYL BRADSHAW

*"I would rather be a little nobody,
than to be an evil somebody."*

—Abraham Lincoln

1

Pippa Holliday bade farewell to the last of her guests and switched off the porch light, pleased her hosting duties had come to an end. She crossed the living room and stepped onto the back deck, pausing to breathe in a lungful of cool coastal air. Nights like this were Pippa's favorite. Nights where she sat with a blanket draped across her legs, listening to the waves slapping against the rocks on the shore below.

Four months earlier Pippa had purchased the oceanfront home in Cambria, California, at a cost of two and a half million dollars, her first big splurge since landing a major acting role on the Netflix series, *A Murderous Affair*. The show was two seasons in, and she'd already been bumped up from supporting actress to lead actress after one of her co-stars entered rehab.

For as long as Pippa could remember, all she had wanted was to become a star. Now, at age twenty-seven, her dreams had become a reality. Life was good, and it seemed to just keep getting better.

With her dinner party at an end, Pippa's thoughts turned to her four-year-old son Cooper. It had been a while since she last peeked in on him. She walked to his room, pulled the blanket over his tiny frame, and brushed a lock of his dark-brown hair out of his face. Leaning down, she planted a kiss on his forehead, and then she watched him sleep, reminiscing about the day she'd discovered she was pregnant.

Back then, Pippa was a broke, out-of-work actress, crashing at friends' apartments and scraping pennies together to get by. She remembered how scared she'd been and how ill-equipped she'd felt about becoming a mother. At the time, she wasn't sure she could manage it. Then her sister Greer swooped in, and everything changed. Greer moved Pippa into her house and looked after Cooper while Pippa pursued a future in Hollywood.

A lifetime ago, and sometimes it still didn't seem real. But it *was* real. At long last, life was the way she'd always imagined it could be.

Pippa tiptoed out of Cooper's room, catching a glimpse of herself in the hallway mirror. Her eyeliner was smudged, and the curls she'd rolled into her long, blond hair had flattened. At some point during the night, she'd also managed to spill a dime-size dollop of tomato sauce on the sleeve of her shirt.

Nice.

Hoping the stain hadn't set, she headed for the laundry room, stopping when she heard a strange noise on the back deck. It sounded like footsteps, like someone was walking around out there, but when she poked her head out to check, she saw no one.

"Hello? Is anyone out here?"

Of course, no one's out there.

You're two stories up, and everyone's gone.

Don't be silly.

Pippa's cat brushed across her leg, and she picked him up, turning him around to face her. "Was it you, hmm? Are you the one making a racket out here, Percy?"

The cat meowed in response, and Pippa smiled, stroking his fur before putting him back down again. Percy trotted off toward Cooper's room, perhaps to jump on the bed and snuggle next to him like he always did.

Pippa removed her shirt, dabbed it with stain remover, and then set it on the counter, leaving it to marinate until morning. Then she wiped her makeup off with a washcloth and slipped into a bikini.

Entering the kitchen a few minutes later, she grabbed a bottle of chardonnay out of the refrigerator. Every night since she'd moved into the new place, Pippa's ritual was the same. She poured herself a glass of wine, got into the pool, and watched the moonlight dance across the ocean. But tonight was different than other nights. The sky had been impregnated with a foggy haze, shielding the moon from view.

Pippa sipped her wine, drifting to one end of the pool and back again. Minutes passed, the fog began to clear, and Pippa's gaze fell upon a dark shape next to the sliding glass door. She could have sworn the shape had moved at first, but not so much now. She swam over to get a closer look, squinting at the area in question. She saw nothing and decided her exhausted mind was playing tricks on her. It had been a long night, and she was beyond tired. Maybe all she needed was a good night's rest.

She tipped the last bit of wine into her mouth and reached for the metal bar to pull herself out of the pool but struggled when her muscles failed her. She tried again, feeling paralyzed, like she was about to collapse.

On her third try, Pippa managed to pull herself onto the cement. She tried to stand and couldn't. Hunched over on all fours, she began crawling toward the house. If she could get to her cell phone, she could call for help. But her cell phone was at least thirty feet away, and with each passing moment, she felt weaker, her stream of consciousness wavering.

Just stop, rest a minute, and try again.

Pippa rolled onto her back and stared up the sky, wondering why her body was so feeble. The sensations she was experiencing were unfamiliar, and she couldn't recall a time when she'd lost control of her body and mind the way she was now.

The wind whistled a faint melody through the air. Pippa listened to it for a moment, and then something dawned on her—it wasn't the wind at all.

Someone was whistling a familiar tune.

Someone close by.

"Relax, Pippa. Close your eyes and relax," a voice said.

She attempted to turn her head toward the voice but couldn't.

Footsteps approached, fast and heavy, and then a blur of a person leaned over her body, blinking at her and smiling. "Don't worry, Pippa. This will all be over in a few minutes."

Two weeks later

Today felt like an all-black kind of day, so I indulged the mood, choosing to dress in a wide-legged jumpsuit and a pair of art deco earrings. While simple, it was still '30s chic. I grabbed a notebook and a pen and answered the door, exchanging formalities with Greer Holliday, my first potential client as a private investigator. I offered her a glass of water, and we sat at the table.

I drummed my fingernails on the tabletop, waiting for her to speak. Judging by the number of times she'd fiddled with the loose button on her shirt, she was nervous—and becoming even more so with each passing second. I wasn't the type of person who could endure uncomfortable silences for long, so I broke it.

"On the phone you said you'd like to hire me. You didn't say why."

Greer's eyes darted around. She twirled a finger around a lock of her long ash-blond hair and said, "I guess I'm just a bit shocked. Your office is, well, not what I expected. I mean, it's not even an office. It's a … you know."

The way she'd said it sounded like we were meeting inside a rundown fixer-upper from the '70s, instead of a cute, top-of-the-line RV. At present, my office was an Airstream—an Airstream parked next to a five-million-dollar house I shared with Giovanni Luciana, my boyfriend.

"I thought about renting a space downtown, but this is just as intimate and private," I said. "Truth is, it doesn't matter where we meet. What matters is being great at my job, and I am."

Greer raised a brow, staring at me like she wanted me to prove it. "How long have you been a private detective?"

"Six months" wouldn't sound too impressive, so I tried wooing her a different way. "I worked as a detective for the San Luis Obispo Police Department for over a decade before I became a private eye."

"Why don't you work there anymore? Did something happen?"

I considered her question, envisioning three metaphorical doors in front of me that, in combination, explained what happened. Behind door number one was my stepfather, Harvey, who was also my former boss. When he retired as chief of police several months ago, I knew working for the department would never be the same again. Behind door number two was Ivan Blackwell, a.k.a. Ivan the Terrible, San Luis Obispo's new chief of police, and a man who was callous, racist, sexist, and with whom I didn't get along. And then there was door number three. Behind it was me, a woman of forty-four who wasn't ready to retire or stop going after bad guys yet.

"Here's what you need to know about me," I said. "I'll work harder for you than anyone else will. I'll solve your case, *and* I'm local. I'm the only private detective in Cambria. Now, let me take a stab at why you're here. Your last name is Holliday, which also happens to be the same last name as Pippa Holliday, the actress who was murdered a couple of weeks back. I assume you'd like to hire me to look into what happened to her and why."

She blinked at me, seemed impressed. "I … yeah. I do. It's just, I've been to the police department a zillion times since she died, and they're worthless. They keep assuring me they're following up on leads. If they are, they're not sharing any information with me. It's frustrating. I need someone to keep me in the loop, someone who will tell me what's going on."

"I get it."

"*Do you?*"

More than she realized.

"How's Cooper doing, your sister's son?" I asked.

She smiled like she was pleased I knew the kiddo's name. "He's confused. Slept through his mother's murder, I guess. Doesn't remember a thing. He keeps asking me when mommy's coming home. I wish I knew what to say, but I don't."

"Where does he think his mother is?"

"I told him Pippa's in heaven. He doesn't understand what heaven is—or where it is, for that matter. Pippa never talked to him about things like that. We weren't raised with religion."

"Where is Cooper now?"

"Preschool. I thought it was best to keep his routine consistent while all of this is going on."

"Which preschool?"

"Horizons Academy."

"What's their security like?"

"Why?"

What an ignorant question.

"Until you know who murdered your sister, you don't know if he's safe."

"The way I look at it, if the killer wanted to take him, he could have the night my sister died."

She had a point.

Then again, maybe the murderer didn't know Cooper was there at the time.

I didn't like the idea of a preschool being responsible for keeping tabs on a child whose mother's killer hadn't been caught.

And ... what if he had seen something and hadn't mentioned it yet?

"Is Cooper staying with you?" I asked.

Greer nodded.

"Where's the boy's father?"

"I have no idea where he is or who he is. Pippa told me they dated for a couple of weeks before he shipped out overseas with the military. It was nothing more than a fling. The pregnancy was an accident."

"Did Pippa ever tell Cooper's dad about him?"

"I don't think so. After the guy shipped out, he never contacted her again, so she decided to raise him on her own. Well, not just on her own. She always had me."

"What about other men in her life?" I asked. "Was she dating anyone else before she died?"

"Pippa didn't have time for anyone else. She was too focused on her acting career. The only male in her life was her son."

"Has the autopsy come back yet?"

"It has, and the medical examiner said she was poisoned."

The county medical examiner was Silas Crowe, a laid-back, yet responsible beach bum I'd worked with for years.

"Poisoned with what?" I asked.

"Rohypnol."

It made me wonder if someone at the house party had drugged her.

And if so, why?

Rohypnol was a popular date-rape drug, which led me to question whether the intention had been to rape her, kill her, or both. The night of Pippa's murder, she'd hosted a private party to celebrate wrapping the previous season of *A Murderous Affair*. The party's guest list included a smattering of people. According to the news reports, Pippa's costar Donovan Grant was the last to leave, exiting the party with his wife. The following morning,

Greer came by to help her sister clean up. She found Pippa next to the pool, dead.

"Was your sister sexually assaulted?"

"No."

If rape wasn't the goal, killing her must have been.

"Can you give me the names of everyone who attended Pippa's party?" I asked.

"I can."

"Were you there the night of the party?"

"For a short time. I left right after I put Cooper to bed."

This was new information, something I didn't know. The local news had mentioned Donovan Grant, his wife, and a few others, but had reported nothing about Greer being in attendance.

"How long were you at your sister's house?" I asked.

"I helped her set up for the party, and then I stayed for the first hour and a half until it was Cooper's bedtime."

"Did anything happen at the party while you were there? Any tension or anyone upset with Pippa for whatever reason?"

She shook her head. "It was perfect. Everyone had a great time, from my perspective, at least."

"Can you describe what you saw the morning you found her?"

She resumed fiddling with the button until the stitching came undone, the button sliding onto the floor. She reached down to grab it, shoved it into her pocket, and then looked at me like she was embarrassed.

"I know how hard it is to lose someone you care about," I said. "Take all the time you need."

"It's just ... it was awful, finding her body. I still can't talk about it."

"No problem. I can get additional information from the medical examiner. Where was Cooper when you arrived?"

"In his room, playing with toys. He seemed to think Pippa was asleep. I don't think he'd left his room that morning."

There was still a chance he'd seen something.

For his sake, I hoped he hadn't.

"You worked for Pippa, didn't you?" I asked.

"I was her assistant."

"You two would have spent a lot of time together, then. Is there anyone in Pippa's life who had a problem with her?"

Greer crossed her arms, considering the question. "I mean, she got along with almost everyone, but yeah … I can think of a couple of people. Laney St. James, for starters."

"Pippa's co-star, right?"

Greer nodded. "She thought she'd do a quick stint in rehab while the show was on hiatus and return for the next season, like the complete meltdown she had on set never happened. Truth is the show's producers had been irritated with her diva attitude for a long time. As soon as she entered rehab, she was fired."

"How did Laney take the news?"

"Not well. She called everyone and cussed them out, even Pippa, who had nothing to do with Laney being fired."

Pippa had been given Laney's job.

It was reason enough.

"How did Pippa respond when Laney lashed out?" I asked.

"She bawled her eyes out. She'd idolized Laney for years. I drove to Laney's house and gave her a piece of my mind. She never said a word to Pippa again."

It was obvious Greer took on a protective role when it came to her sister and that she was the more dominant of the two.

"Who else had a problem with your sister?" I asked.

"Trevor Armstrong. They dated for about six months. She liked him, but it didn't last because he's a paranoid weirdo."

"Paranoid in what way?"

"On most Sunday's, Pippa and I had brunch together. There was this one time when Pippa had just arrived, and her cell phone rang. It was Trevor."

"What did he say?"

"He'd stayed over at her place the night before, and he was calling to say he thought she was too dressed up to be having brunch with her sister. He accused her of lying to him about her plans for the day. He didn't come right out and say he thought she might have some other guy on the side, but that's what he was suggesting. Pippa would never cheat on anyone. She wasn't that kind of person."

A jealous coworker. A jealous ex. A pattern was beginning to form.

"I'm assuming you've told all of this to the police," I said.

"Yep. Everything, including the phone calls I discovered on Pippa's phone."

"What phone calls?"

"Dozens of them from Trevor, all in the last five or six weeks of her life."

"How long were the calls?"

She shrugged. "I didn't go over every single one, but it varied. Some were a few minutes. Others were longer."

"She was talking to him before she died, then."

"Or he was trying to talk to her."

I turned to a blank page in the notebook and flipped it around, handing her the pen. "Write down the names of the party's guests for me, as well as Trevor's information. I'll start there."

She spent the next few minutes complying with my request and then returned the notebook and pen to me. "Anything else?"

"I'll also need to take a look around your sister's place."

"I can get you a key, but it's still considered a crime scene. They haven't let me back since I packed Cooper's things."

Pippa's house would have to wait for now.

In the meantime …

"I'd also like to speak to Cooper, sooner than later," I said.

"But I haven't committed to hiring you yet."

I crossed my arms and smiled. "Are you sure? Seems to me like you just did."

3

just quit."

I stood in the Airstream's doorway, staring down at a fuming Lilia Hunter. The look on her face told me she was seconds away from a full-blown panic attack. She ran a hand through her hair and bit down on her lip like she was trying not to cry.

"It's going to be all right. I'll get you a glass of water, and we can talk. Okay?"

She shimmied her backpack off her shoulder, unzipped it, and pulled out a bottle of red wine. "Thanks, but water is not going to cut it today. I need something a lot stronger."

I swung the door all the way open. "Sure, come on in."

Hunter walked past me, flopped down at the table, and buried her head in her hands. Luka, my Samoyed, meandered his way over to her, staring up at me like he wanted to help but didn't know how. He settled on nestling at her feet.

A few years earlier, when I'd taken some time away from detective work after my daughter's unexpected death, Hunter had been promoted to detective, a job she didn't relish. When I returned, she tried to step down, but I convinced her to stay on as the department's office manager. She had also moonlighted with me from time to time, assisting me with research on my homicide cases. She was smart and capable, a lot more capable than she realized.

I popped the cork and poured the wine, handing the wineglass to Hunter as I sat across from her. She downed half of it and said, "Please have some. I brought it for both of us."

It wasn't even noon yet.

Still, I didn't want to offend her while she was in such a fragile state.

"Oh, thanks," I said. "Maybe I'll have a glass in a bit. What happened at work? I assume Blackwell had something to do with your abrupt departure?"

She knocked back more of her drink and nodded. "He had *everything* to do with it. The jerk treats me like I'm a bug stuck to the bottom of his shoe."

"You lasted a lot longer than I thought you would."

"Yeah, well, I've wanted to quit ever since you did. I just couldn't bring myself to do it."

"What changed your mind?"

"The moment he passed by my desk this morning, he started giving me a lecture, just like he does every morning when he comes in. He always finds something to harass or criticize me about. Except today, instead of saying sorry to him or promising to do better, I thought about you and how you stood up to him all those months ago. It was so badass, and I decided it was time to stand up for myself and stop allowing people like him to treat me like garbage. So, yeah, I quit."

I reached over, giving her arm a squeeze. "Good for you! Did you get to tell him off before you left at least?"

She stared down at Luka. "Kinda. I wrote him a nasty letter and left it on his desk."

It was a lot different than the way I'd handled things on my last day, but a letter was still something, and I was proud of her for it. "I'm glad you don't work for him anymore. He doesn't deserve you. He never did."

"I feel like an idiot for waiting so long."

"It doesn't matter how long it took to get you to the place where you are now. What matters is ... you're here. You did it. You left a toxic environment. Give yourself some credit."

She shrugged. "Guess you're right."

"What now? Any ideas on what you're going to do next?"

She slid her empty glass to the side and blinked at me. "I, ahh, well ... I do have *one* idea. I'm just not sure what you'll think of it."

"Let's hear it."

"I was, umm, hoping I could come work for you on the regular. We've always worked well together, haven't we? I can see it now. You take on the bad guys, and I assist. I'll be the Robin to your Batman. Or no. Even better, I'll be the Alfred to your Batman, working behind the scenes to help you solve crimes."

Her suggestion to work together was unexpected and caught me off-guard. I didn't want to let her down, but I'd just taken my first case, and money wasn't rolling in—not yet. And I'd been looking forward to being a one-woman show. I wasn't sure I wanted to work with anyone else, even if it was someone as reliable and worthy as Hunter.

"I hadn't thought about taking on anyone yet," I said. "Even if I did, I'm not sure I could afford you. I've just taken my first case."

She grinned like she'd anticipated my response. "You know how I said I'd been thinking about quitting for a while? I've also been planning for it—saving, scheming. I have my private-investigator license and everything."

I'd never been one for surprises, and I found myself wishing she would have told me sooner. Perhaps I should have indulged in a glass of wine before the conversation got going. "Oh…kay. What are you thinking?"

"You take on murder cases, and I'll continue to assist, gathering information just like I did when you worked for the department. In the meantime, to bring in my own money, I could take on things you have no interest in—like finding someone's long-lost grandfather, staking out cheating spouses, running background checks."

I ran a hand along my chin, considering what she'd just said. It wasn't a bad idea. Until now, I'd always assumed I'd work alone. It was possible I needed to expand my vision.

I poured her a little more wine and said, "Tell you what … Give me a little time to think about it, okay?"

4

Silas Crowe had his hands wrapped around a coffee cup when I joined him at his booth at the Hungry Hummingbird. He eyed the drink I'd just picked up at the coffee bar, grinned at me, and said, "What did *you* get?"

"Small nonfat mocha, light foam, no whip."

He shot me a confused glance. "Sounds, ahh ... complicated."

I lifted my cup to my lips. "It's good. Want to try it?"

"Nope, I'll stick to my hot cocoa, full fat, extra whip."

I laughed and pulled my emerald-green, wool princess coat around me a little tighter. "It's colder than usual for the end of February, isn't it? Overcast and cloudy. Supposed to be like this all week."

"Tell me about it. Been waiting for a good swell so I can hop back on my surfboard again."

"Did you hear Hunter quit the department today?"

"Sure did. It's all anyone is talking about."

"She stopped by my place earlier," I said.

"How's she doing?"

"Get this—she wants to work together like we did when I worked for the department."

"I thought murder investigations gave her panic attacks."

"They do. She wants to stay on the sidelines, gathering information for me. And she wants to take on her own cases, ones that *don't* involve dead people. Well … *not* the kind of dead people I investigate anyway."

"Sounds like a great idea to me. You gonna do it?"

"Maybe. I told her I'd think about it."

Although I was enjoying our casual exchange, I had a feeling he knew why I'd asked for this meetup. Since I no longer worked for the police department, I needed to find a backdoor into Pippa's murder investigation, and I hoped Silas was it.

"I accepted my first murder investigation this morning," I said.

He held his cup in the air and said, "Cool. Lemme guess … Greer Holliday hired you."

"She did. How did you know?"

"I've talked to her a couple of times. I know she's frustrated about how the case is going. She thinks we're holding things back from her."

"Are you?"

"Not by choice. Blackwell asked us to keep things quiet until we know more about her sister's murder."

I wondered what they knew that I didn't.

Time to find out.

"About that … I was hoping you'd agree to talk to me about her case," I said. "I don't want to get you into trouble though. I know Blackwell wouldn't approve if he found out you were sharing her autopsy results or information about the crime scene with me."

Silas ran a hand through his wavy, shoulder-length hair. "I like most people. But, man, I can't stand that guy. I wish Harvey hadn't retired. He gave me space to do my thing. Blackwell's always around, looking over my shoulder, acting like he knows more about postmortem examinations than I do."

"I can imagine."

"Speaking of dudes I'd rather avoid … you meet Foley yet?"

"Who's Foley?"

"Rex Foley is the new detective—your replacement."

I shook my head. "What's he like?"

"A mini version of Blackwell. A smug, loud overachiever."

Great.

One Blackwell was enough.

"As long as he doesn't get in my way, we'll be fine," I said.

Silas smacked his hand against mine, giving me a high-five. "That's my girl. Truth is, Foley can be a decent guy. I've seen it. He acts one way when he's around Blackwell, and another way when he isn't."

"He's new. Maybe he's working overtime to impress Blackwell. If he is, he's wasting his time. There's no impressing that guy."

"I agree. What do you want to know about the Holliday case?"

"Walk me through the autopsy. What did you find? What do you know so far? I heard Pippa was drugged. Rohypnol, right? I always thought roofies were associated with loss of coordination, dizziness, confusion, and that type of thing. Not death."

He leaned back, crossed his arms, and nodded. "Depends on the dosage. I'm sure you're aware the stuff is banned. If it was bought on the black market, hard to know how strong those pills are."

"How many pills are we talking?"

"My estimate? Five or six. Maybe more. Found traces of it in the wineglass next to the pool and in the wine bottle itself."

"Do we know if the wine was left over from the party?"

He shook his head. "It wasn't. Greer told us Pippa drank a specific type of wine each night while she swam. And I guess she had sensitive teeth, so she'd take it out of the fridge about thirty minutes before she drank it, remove the lid, and let it sit for a bit."

"If she opened it after the party, I assume the killer knew her routine and waited in the house for her to open the wine and then drink it."

"I was thinkin' the same thing."

There was a good reason why rohypnol was a popular date-rape drug. It was odorless, tasteless, and colorless. It also didn't take long to kick in, making it the perfect drug for the predators of the world.

"What was her time of death?"

"When her sister found her, I guessed she'd been dead about twelve hours. She was in full rigor when I got to her—stiff muscles, flexed knees and elbows, crooked fingers—you know the deal."

"Were you able to lift prints off the wine bottle or her glass?"

He nodded. "All Pippa's."

He smacked his lips together, something he often did before he spilled juicy information.

"What is it?" I asked.

"There's, ahh … there's something which hasn't been released to the public yet. The crime scene was staged."

"How so?"

"Victim's hands were placed one on top of the other over her heart. And get this …"

He reached inside his pocket, pulled out his cell phone, flipped through several photos, and then turned the phone around so I could see. I blinked, staring at what appeared to be a snippet of white paper with the number 1 written in the center in red.

"Where did you find it?"

"Stuck to the side of a lounge chair near the pool."

"And you think the killer left it?"

"Pippa's head was turned to the side, facing the piece of paper."

"Anything else I should know?"

"A lock of hair was missing, around a three-inch chunk."

I crossed one leg over the other.

"Those wheels of yours are turning," Silas said. "I can tell. What are you thinking?"

I was thinking the crime scene reminded me of something— or rather, *someone*.

"What has Blackwell said about it?" I asked.

"Not much aside from threatening everyone to keep the details under wraps until he says otherwise. Why?"

If Blackwell didn't know the significance behind the staged crime scene, I had a leg up, for now.

I stood. "Thank you for trusting me with this information, Silas. I'd like to stay longer, but I need to stop by and see Harvey."

"Why? What's going on?"

I slung my handbag over my shoulder and remained at the table a moment, tapping my shoe on the ground. "I want to share something with you. If I do, it needs to be kept between us for now. I realize it's a big ask. If it makes you uncomfortable, I don't have to tell—"

He waved a hand, stopping me. "You can tell me anything, Gigi. You may not work for the department anymore, but my allegiance is and always will be to you. Besides, we're buddies. Aren't we?"

"We are."

He rubbed his hands together. "Alrighty then, what's up?"

"When I first made detective, I went through all of my father's old cases. In some ways, I think it made me feel closer to him—knowing I was doing the same job he did before he died. One case stood out more than the others, a case he worked on in 1985. Female serial killer. Drugged her victims. Left a piece of paper with the number 1 on it at each crime scene. Posed them after death in the same way you just described *and* sliced off a piece of their hair to keep as a souvenir. She's serving a life sentence in Chowchilla."

"How many victims?"

"Before she was caught? Eight, if I remember right. They were all found, but get this ... when she was arrested, she swore she'd killed *nine* women, not eight. Problem is, there were no other missing women in the area that matched her MO, and she wouldn't give up the name of the ninth victim."

Silas smacked a hand on the table. "Whoa. You're thinking what I'm thinking, right?"

I nodded. "It's possible we're dealing with a copycat killer."

5

found Harvey sitting in a chair on the back deck, reading today's paper. Splashed across the front was a photo of Pippa along with the headline: *No New Leads in The Holliday Case.*

Harvey glanced up at me and pointed at Pippa's photo. "Shame about the Holliday woman, isn't it? I liked the television show she starred in. Wonder what they'll do without her."

I took a seat next to him. "She's the reason I'm here. Her sister just hired me to investigate Pippa's murder."

He raised a brow. "Oh?"

Before I had the chance to utter another word, my mother burst onto the deck carrying a tray of mugs filled to the brim with coffee. She gave each of us a mug, then plopped down beside me, something I'd hoped she wouldn't do but assumed she would.

Six months earlier, Harvey had suffered a heart attack one night during family dinner. It was the reason he'd retired as the city's police chief years earlier than he'd planned. Ever since, my mother steered us kids away from any conversation she believed would cause him even the smallest amount of stress. This included most conversations like the one I hoped to have with him now.

My mother draped an arm around me and gave me a quick squeeze. "What brings you by? Seems like we haven't seen you in ages."

If her definition of *ages* meant not since the Sunday dinner a couple of weeks ago, then yes, I suppose it had been.

"She's taken on her first case," Harvey beamed.

Uh-oh.

"Ooh, what kind of case?" my mother asked.

I scrolled through a mental list of possible answers and realized there wasn't one that didn't give away the nature of the beast.

Short on patience, my mother waved a hand in front of me. "Wait! Don't tell me. Let me guess. Hmm … all right, I've got it! Your client was adopted and wants you to find his, or her, birth mother. Or, oh, hang on … you were hired to look for someone's long-lost love. Am I right? How'd I do?"

"It's, ahh, none of those things. It's a murder investigation."

My mother's eyes widened. "*Murder?* Not the poor girl from the paper, right?"

Harvey gave me a look that suggested I hold off on saying too much more, so I did.

In the meantime, he jumped in. "Aren't you going to be late for Pilates class, honey?"

She swished a hand through the air. "It's not every day Georgiana comes by, is it? Perhaps I'll skip class today, just this one time."

He sat back, seemed to be thinking on her response, then tried again. "I thought you and Beth were meeting up for class and going to dinner afterward."

My mother grunted, "Oh, shoot, you're right. I'd almost forgotten. I guess I better get going." She turned toward me. "How long will you be here?"

"Not long. I'll stop by another day, okay?"

I hoped my reply was enough to pacify her.

It was not.

She stood and walked away, mumbling, "That's what you always say, and then I don't see you for weeks."

Harvey and I made small talk for a few minutes until my mother's car pulled out of the driveway and the garage door closed. When we were sure she was gone, he wagged a finger at me and grinned. "All right! Tell me *all* about your new case, and don't you dare leave anything out. This is the most excitement I've had in months."

I filled him in on everything I knew, and then I started in on my theory. "I'm familiar with all of my dad's old cases. You worked that serial killer case with him in the '80s, didn't you?"

"I did. It was, well, unbelievable at the time. For months we thought we were searching for a man. Imagine our surprise when the killer turned out to be a woman. Not too common for a serial murderer, then *or* now."

"Based on what I know so far, I believe Pippa's murder mirrors some of the same things that happened back then."

He nodded. "Similar enough. Your line of thinking has merit. When it comes to a copycat though, you could be looking at a man or a woman. Hard to say. Just because it was a woman before doesn't mean it's a woman now."

"What can you tell me about her—Atticus Wolfe?"

"Oh, let's see now. For starters, she was sweet on your father, flirted with him every chance she got. She was an absolute stunner. I think that's what lured people in—both men *and* women. She wasn't like most serial killers back in those days. That's why she was so hard to profile at first."

"How was she different?"

"She was tall, slender, well-dressed, charming. She graduated from a prestigious university in California and made decent money working as an anesthesiologist. She lived in a nice neighborhood, had nice parents, and she was married to a kind young man who was the principal at the local school. He had no idea about the kind of woman he'd married, and when we told him, he refused to believe it."

"Even *after* she was convicted?"

Wow.

Talk about devotion.

He rubbed a hand across his forehead and shrugged. "Dunno how anyone could stay with a cold-blooded killer."

"Are they still married now?"

"Not anymore, no. He stayed by her side, oh, for about ten years, I'd say. Then he killed himself. Must have been hard. People recognized him everywhere he went."

"Poor guy."

"I'll never forget what she said to me the day she was hauled off to prison. We were escorting her to the transfer bus, and she looked me dead in the eye and said: 'I bet you think the wolf has been silenced. One day, she'll rise again. And I hope you're still alive to see it.'"

Feisty, in a creepy *person-no-one-wants-to-meet-in-a-dark-alley* kind of way.

"I wonder if I can get access to see her," I said. "Boyd Jackson is still the prison warden, right?"

"He is." Harvey grabbed his cell phone off the table and scrolled through his contacts. "I might be able to help. Let me make a call."

6

When Harvey handed me his cell phone, Warden Jackson started the conversation with, "Detective Germaine, I hear you've gone rogue."

"I've started my own private-investigator business," I said. "Just accepted my first case."

"Congrats. Does your new chief of police know yet?"

"If Blackwell doesn't, he's about to find out."

"Harvey tells me you'd like to visit Atticus Wolfe in relation to a case you're working on. Why?"

"There are similarities to the murder I'm investigating, and those Atticus committed in the '80s."

"Similarities like what?"

I paused, thinking about what to say next.

For now, I wanted to keep most of the finer, more intimate details to myself.

"Positioning of the victim, that kind of thing," I said.

"I'm going to need a bit more information."

"Some things haven't been released to the press yet. I'm hesitant to reveal too much at this point."

He breathed a long, hard sigh. "You can trust me, Germaine. If you want to see her, I need to know what I'm dealing with, all right? It'll stay between us. Okay?"

Warden Jackson was a man Harvey trusted.

I hoped I could do the same.

I filled him in on most of what I knew so far.

When I finished, he said, "A copycat, huh? Wonder if you're right. When did you want to see her?"

"As soon as I can."

"Even if I were to grant you access, she may not want to see you. And that's up to her. She's not keen on visitors. Hasn't been for years."

"Tell her my father was one of the detectives who worked on her case."

"I doubt she'll care after all this time."

"Harvey said she was sweet on him. I'm hoping it's enough to make her consider seeing me, at least."

"Say she does agree … you need to set your expectation bar low. She's a different person now. Perfect behavior, well-liked, honest. Not sure your murder investigation is something she'll want to talk about."

"All I can do is try."

He grunted a passive, "Yeah, suppose you're right. Give me some time. I'll call you back."

7

Laney St. James came to the door the following morning dressed in a long, pink, satin nightgown and a matching pair of feathery, heeled slippers. Her platinum-blond hair was pulled back into a bun, and she looked even skinnier in person than she did on television. It wasn't a good skinny either. It was a frail, unwell skinny, like the slightest gust of wind could bowl her over.

Laney blinked at me, brought the cigarette between her fingers to her lips, and took a puff, blowing the smoke in my general direction. "Didn't you see the sign outside the gate?"

"The one that says *No Trespassing*? Yeah. Your gate was open."

She shook her head, huffing a rigid, "How many times do I have to tell him? It's like there's no brain inside that head of his. And I keep falling for it. Want some advice? Don't ever hire family to do what a professional should do. It's not worth it."

"Okay. Thanks?"

"Who are you, and why are you ringing my doorbell at nine o'clock in the morning?"

"My name's Georgiana Germaine, and I'm investigating the death of Pippa Holliday. I'd like to ask you a few questions. Can I come in?"

"I've already talked to a detective. And I never adult before noon."

She slammed the door in my face, leaving me standing there, stunned. It seemed the reputation she'd earned in Hollywood was an accurate one.

And since I'd decided to fly over to see her instead of making the drive from Cambria to Hollywood, I wasn't ready to give up yet.

I left and returned at 12:02 with a small offering in hand.

"Is that coffee for me?" she asked.

I nodded. "I hear it's the best in the city."

I handed it to her, and she forced a smile, waving me inside. "You have fifteen minutes, and then I have a call with my agent."

"I'll take it."

She walked down the hallway, stopping a moment to turn back, look me up and down, and say, "Love the duds, by the way."

Today I was dressed in a pair of 1930s trousers with gold button accents on the waist, a burgundy, satin, sailor-style shirt, and a linen cloche hat.

We sat across from each other on a pair of black-velvet chairs, and I glanced around, my eyes coming to rest on a stack of books on the coffee table. The stack included a memoir on Bette Davis, a diet book on intermittent fasting, *and* something which caught my eye—a hardback book about female serial killers.

I picked up the serial-killer book and thumbed through it, noting several excerpts throughout had been highlighted in yellow marker. "You interested in serial killers?"

She stubbed her cigarette out in an ashtray. "Isn't everyone?"

"Not everyone marks up the pages of a book on serial killers."

"What's your point?"

I put a pin in the topic of conversation and moved on. "How would you describe your relationship with Pippa?"

"I wouldn't."

"Why not?"

She tapped a long, pointy fingernail on the armchair. "Do *you* make friends with sneaky little snakes?"

"Depends on the variety of snake."

"My point is ... Pippa slithered her way onto *my* show, and then she stole *my* job."

It was one way of looking at it.

Another way was one I doubted Laney would ever admit. She'd sabotaged her own career, leaving the door wide open for Pippa to stroll in and take her place.

"You were fired," I said.

"And who do you think made that happen?"

She blamed Pippa.

At least she wasn't trying to hide it.

"The night of Pippa's murder, she hosted a dinner party," I said.

"Oh, I know. Donovan Grant called me after he left and told me all about it. He said it was a real snorefest."

"What else did he say?"

"Not much. He was tired. We weren't on the phone long."

"Where were *you* the night Pippa died?" I asked.

"Why does it matter?"

"The murderer hasn't been caught yet."

"And I suppose you think *I* had something to do with it, just like the detective who paid me a visit last week."

I leaned forward, looking her in the eye. "I think revenge is as good a motive as any."

"Revenge is the perfect motive. In my case, it would be a bit obvious, wouldn't it? Everyone knew how I felt about her in the end. Besides, I'm trying to get my career on track. Why would I put a target on my back? I'm not a flipping idiot."

"Idiot or not, it doesn't mean you're innocent."

"It doesn't mean I'm guilty either." She glanced at an expensive-looking gold-plated clock on the mantel. "My meeting is in five minutes. Time for you to go."

I nodded, ordered an Uber, and walked toward the door. "You still haven't said where you were that night. Do you have an alibi, anyone who can prove you weren't at Pippa's house when she died?"

"I don't need an alibi. I didn't do it. And don't come back. I won't speak to you again if you do."

I faced her. "You know, there are a lot of things I'm not good at. But detective work, solving crimes—those two areas I excel in."

She clapped her hands. "Good for you."

"I tried going easy on you today. I played nice, gave you the chance to let yourself off the hook. Cooperate with me or don't. But know this—since you've chosen not to answer the question, I'll now be forced to dig up every bit of information on you I can find. Your past, your present. The good, the bad, the stuff you thought you'd buried ... but not deep enough."

She stepped onto the porch and narrowed her eyes. "Go ahead. Dig. I don't care."

"People *like* talking about other people, and when they talk to me about you, I'm not so sure it will be good for the life you're trying to breathe back into your career." I tipped my hat. "Enjoy the rest of your day, Miss St. James."

She stood, hands on hips, seething like she was trying to decide whether to head back to the house or come after me. I walked toward the car, allowing her to digest my words. Before I made it to the curb, she yelled, "Wait!"

Laney held up a finger, went back inside, and reemerged less than a minute later. She charged toward me, waving a stack of papers in her hand.

"Yeah? What is it?"

"Dig into my past all you want. It's just …"

"It's just what?"

She eyeballed the driver like she worried he might eavesdrop on our conversation even though his windows were up and he was facing the opposite direction.

"I had a date the night Pippa died," she said. "A date with a high-profile man who isn't divorced yet."

"His name?"

"I'll tell you the same thing I told the last detective who came to see me. I'm not giving his name. Not to him, not to you."

"Don't you want to rule yourself out as a suspect?"

"It's not worth it. He'd kill me." She paused, as if thinking about the words she'd just used. "I mean, he wouldn't *kill me*. You get that, right? He'd be angry with me though. We can't go public with our relationship, not until his divorce is final."

"When will that be?"

"I don't know. Hollywood divorces are messy. Soon. He promised."

"How do you know he's divorcing his wife?"

"He told me."

The man could say anything.

Talk was cheap.

And Laney was rich.

Maybe all he was after was her money. Then again, she'd said he was "high profile."

"Has he filed for divorce yet?" I asked.

"He said he has."

"Have you seen the paperwork?"

"Well … no. I don't need to though. I trust him, and he trusts me."

I ripped a piece of paper out of my notebook and jotted down a few things. I handed it to her along with my business card and said, "In the state of California, all aspects of a divorce are public record. You can find out what he's filed at the California Department of Public Health. I've written the website down on that piece of paper for you."

"I don't need to find out anything. He wouldn't lie to me."

"It wouldn't hurt to check it out, for your own peace of mind more than anything. You're going out of your way to protect him, even though you know you're a suspect. If it were me, I'd want to make sure the same consideration went both ways."

"Fine, I'll think about it. I didn't murder Pippa, and there's no evidence to suggest I did."

"Not yet."

Laney huffed a frustrated sigh and then handed over the stack of papers she was holding. "*This* is the script for a movie I starred in several years ago called *The Killing Hour*. It was my first starring role. I played a serial killer, a black widow who traveled around the country, marrying men and then offing them for insurance money. It's the reason why I'd highlighted all those pages in the book you saw on my coffee table. Trying to get in the mind of a killer doesn't make me one. Whatever you're trying to pin on me … well, pin it on someone else."

8

I had no problem pinning Pippa's murder on someone other than Laney St. James *if* she was innocent. I shelved my suspicions for now and decided to track down Trevor Armstrong, Pippa's alleged jealous ex-boyfriend, who also lived in the Hollywood area. According to Greer, he was a private chef who'd met Pippa a year ago. Since then, he'd opened a restaurant on Sunset Boulevard, a short drive from where I was now.

Enigma was a small eatery with a giant "all-seeing" eye painted on the side of its brick building. A handful of patrons sat outside, sipping on health-conscious drinks and munching away on dishes that resembled glorified rabbit food. I passed each table, glancing at the offerings, scouting for an egg dish of some kind. I didn't see one.

Bummer.

I could do with some eggs today.

Plants of all shapes and sizes were scattered about the café's interior. A bookshelf near the entrance was filled with stacks of board and card games, and cornhole was set up in the back. Most of the café's patrons wore tank tops and hoodies, and cut-off shorts and sandals, even though it was the middle of February.

Chill instrumental music played through speakers overhead, soft and low. It was enough to lull me to sleep if I sat long enough to allow myself to unwind. Before long, I was yawning. I was in desperate need of a pick me up.

"Hello, can I help you?"

I shifted my attention from a large potted plant to the smiling woman behind the counter. She was tall, in her late twenties, and had bright-green eyes and long, light-brown hair, which she wore in a braid over her shoulder. The small, leaf-shaped name badge pinned to her apron read SAMANTHA.

"Can I get a London Fog?" I asked.

"Sure. Anything else?"

"Trevor Armstrong," I said.

She laughed. "He's not on the menu."

"He owns this place, right?"

"He does. He's my dad."

Her dad?

How old is this guy?

"Your dad dated Pippa Holliday," I said.

Her smile faded. "Yeah, for a while."

"Did you like her?"

"Sure, I guess. She was nice."

Her comment didn't match her demeanor.

She seemed agitated.

A diversion was needed.

I pointed to a broken fingernail on her right hand. "It's such a pain when a nail breaks, isn't it? I don't know about you, but I have such a hard time waiting to get it fixed."

Her face flushed, and she tucked the offending hand inside her apron's pocket. "I, uhh … slammed it in the register."

Good one, Georgiana.

Make her feel even less comfortable than she already is.

"I was thinking of taking something to go. What do you recommend?"

"Oh, well, if you like salad, the Green Goddess is the most popular thing on the menu."

"Sure, I'll take one of those. To-go, please."

"No problem."

She started on my drink order, glancing at me every now and then like she had something on her mind—something she wanted to get out.

I waited, hoping if I didn't push her, it would pay off.

And then it did.

"Pippa was just … you know, close to my age. It was weird seeing them together. Why are you asking about her? Are you a cop?"

"I'm a private detective. I'm looking into her murder."

She nodded. "It sucks, what happened to her. Horrible way to die."

"Did you spend any time with Pippa while she was dating your dad?"

"Some. We went to lunch a few times, and she invited me to the set of her television show one day. I was having a great time until her sister showed up."

"What happened?"

"I could tell she didn't like me. Well, not me. My dad. And since I'm his daughter, she must have decided she didn't like me either. We were sitting there, chatting, getting along great. She asked me who I was, and when I told her, her entire body went stiff. She stopped talking to me, acted like I wasn't even there." Samantha handed me my drink. "It will be a few minutes on the salad."

"No problem. Is your father here?"

"Umm, I'm not sure. He was thinking about running some errands a few minutes ago. Let me check."

She left the register and walked through a doorway decorated with long strands of brown beads. I waited. A minute later, a man walked toward me. He was barefoot and sported a loose, gray manbun.

He also carried the aroma of someone who'd been smoking weed.

"You wanted to see me?" he asked.

"You dated Pippa Holliday for a while, didn't you?"

"I did. Why?"

"Do you always date much younger women?"

It was one of those comments I thought I'd keep to myself instead of verbalizing—until I blurted it out.

Oops.

He remained unaffected. "Love is love. What difference does it make?"

Perhaps he was right. They were both adults. Who was I to say what love was and what it wasn't?

"Can we talk?" I asked.

Trevor reached for his cell phone. "I, uhh … sure. I can spare a few minutes."

He ushered me to a back room with beanbag chairs scattered around. He sat on one and motioned for me to do the same.

"Care to tell me who you are and why you're here asking about Pippa?" he asked.

While I explained who I was and the purpose of my visit, he laced his fingers together behind his head, leaning back and kicking his feet up on the cushion next to him. I tried my best to ignore the black grime on the bottom of his feet … and couldn't. It was like they'd been dipped in black paint and then dragged through the dirt.

"I'm glad someone's looking into what happened to Pippa," he said. "The police haven't done squat as far as I'm concerned."

"Investigations like this one take time. Tell me about your relationship with her."

"Pippa was one of the most beautiful people I've ever known. Inside and out."

"Why did the two of you break up?"

"Before we go any further, I'd like to know who hired you."

Fair question.

"Greer Holliday."

"I'm guessing she's the one who suggested me as a suspect."

"I never said you were a suspect."

"You're here, aren't you? What did she tell you about me?"

"It doesn't matter. I'm more interested in who you are and what you have to say."

"For the last five years, I've practiced yoga a few days a week. At first, I did it to ease my overactive imagination, slow things down, learn how to shift focus from one thing to another. I get something in my mind, you see, and once I do, I can't seem to get it out. You ever feel like that?"

Every day.

"Sometimes," I said. "What does it have to do with you and Pippa?"

"I fell harder for her than any woman I've ever dated … and fast. Too fast, I suppose. By our third date, I told her she was the one for me. Three weeks later, I bought her a ring."

Good grief.

Slow the train down, man.

"You bought her an engagement ring?" I asked.

"I wasn't trying to marry her—not right away. I didn't propose or get down on one knee or anything. I just wanted her to know I was committed to a future together."

No wonder Greer saw Trevor the way she did. Sitting here with him now, it was clear he was a ball of hyperactive, impulsive energy.

"How did Pippa feel about receiving a ring so soon after you first started dating?" I asked.

"She was in shock. Didn't expect it. And I'll admit, when she tried to explain her feelings, I wasn't in the right mindset to listen. I took the explanation as a sign of rejection. I could have handled it a lot better than I did."

"What did you do?"

He bowed his head as if embarrassed to face me. "I tossed the ring into the trash and left. I shouldn't have done it. I should have stayed, heard her out. I know that now. Guess I thought she'd find my spontaneity refreshing," he said, making eye contact again. "Most guys aren't in touch with their feelings. I am, and I thought she'd appreciate me for being straightforward about what I wanted and where I saw the two of us going."

"You still haven't told me the reason you two broke up."

"In my opinion, it came down to one thing—trust. I've struggled with it a fair amount in the past. I was single for three years before we met, and I thought I'd worked through the issues I had with other women before her. I was wrong. It was still there, like a bad habit I couldn't shake."

"Why didn't you trust her?" I asked.

"I did trust her. I didn't trust *them*."

"Them?"

"I saw the way other guys looked at her, talked to her when we went out. Men half my age waiting to swoop in and steal her away from me. I rode her about it, even after she went out of her way to convince me she didn't want to be with anyone else."

Sounded like good old-fashioned jealousy to me.

Had his jealousy led to her murder?

"Did you talk to Pippa or see her again after you split up?" I asked.

"I tried. She wouldn't take my calls at first. Then one night after she had a bit to drink, she called me. I told her I'd started going to therapy, and she admitted she was heartbroken over the way things ended between us."

"When did she call you?"

"About six weeks ago, I'd say. The call … it was strange."

"In what way?"

"She kept talking about the past. Over and over, she said if she could go back, if she could have a do-over, it would be different this time. She'd make things right. At first, I thought she meant *our* past, but she didn't. There was something in her own life, something she hadn't made peace with yet. I kept asking, trying to get her to open up to me about it. She wouldn't."

"Did you speak to her again?"

His eyes brimmed with tears. He swallowed hard. "I didn't just speak to her—we started seeing each other again."

It was a revelation I hadn't seen coming.

Greer had mentioned the calls, but nothing about them seeing each other again.

Was it possible she didn't know they'd gotten back together?

"Was Greer aware you were seeing Pippa again?" I asked.

"I'm not sure. Pippa wanted to tell her in her own time. I don't know if she got the chance to do it before she died."

"If you were together again, why weren't you invited to her dinner party?" I asked.

"I asked her the same thing. She said after what we went through the first time, she wanted to take things slow. I didn't like it, but hey, I rocked the boat enough on our first go-round. I just wanted things to be better this time."

"Your daughter didn't like Pippa, did she?"

"They got along fine. She was shocked over our age difference. It was hard for her to take at first, but she was coming around in the end. When I told her we'd started seeing each other again, she was happy for me. She knew how much I'd missed her."

"Where was Samantha the night Pippa died?"

"She was with me. We had dinner together at my place."

"Samantha was with you the entire night?"

"Headed home about ten or eleven. I know where you're going with this, and well, you know it's almost a four-hour drive from here to Pippa's place. Besides, my daughter is a good kid."

And *he* was a convenient alibi.

9

Trevor Armstrong claimed he'd attended the movie *Deep Water* with a friend on the night Pippa died, something I'd verify later. When asked why they didn't speak after Pippa's house party had ended, his answer was simple—he'd fallen asleep waiting for her to call him, and she never did.

I grabbed another Uber and hopped on a flight back home. When I touched ground and had the chance to check my phone, I noticed I'd received a text message from Simone Bonet, a forensic anthropologist and my brother Paul's girlfriend. She wanted to meet. I wanted to melt into the sofa and sip on a glass of prosecco, watching something on TV while sandwiched between Giovanni and Luka.

After suggesting we get together the next night instead, she managed to talk me into grabbing one drink, promising she'd send me on my way after that. If there was one thing I knew about Simone, she was a talker. The odds I'd make it home at a decent hour were slim. Still, I relented. Something in the tone of her voice piqued my interest.

Simone arrived at Starfish Beach Bar dressed in a Morrissey T-shirt beneath a burgundy blazer and a pair of black jeans, which were rolled up at the bottom to show off her matching Converse footwear. She got out of her car and ran toward me, her long, dark, wavy locks bouncing in the wind. She looked like a dressed-down, yet stylish version of Kerry Washington.

Simone wrapped her arms around me, took a few steps back, and wiggled her fingers in front of my face. "Check it out!"

I leaned in for a closer look at the big, shiny engagement ring on her wedding finger, which came as a bit of a shock. The first time my brother proposed, Simone said she needed more time. Seemed he'd asked again, and this time, she'd accepted.

"It's gorgeous," I said. "When did he pop the question?"

"Last night, on the beach. We were having a picnic. He pointed at what I thought was some random bottle that had washed ashore. I grabbed it, and when I opened it, a ring slipped out, along with a letter he'd written me."

"I had no idea my brother was so creative," I said.

She looped her arm around mine and smiled. "Me either."

We headed inside and took a seat at the bar.

"I knew something was up," I said. "You sounded a little different than usual on the phone."

We ordered a couple of drinks and she said, "Yeah ... about sounding different on the phone. I, uhh, I did something today I shouldn't have done. Rex Foley stopped by the lab ... you know, the new detective Blackwell hired."

"What's he like?"

"He wasn't around long enough for me to get a read on him. He was talking about the case and the fact Hunter had just quit. He asked about you, and whether you were the person Blackwell made you out to be, and I, ahh, well ..."

Told him what I was up to nowadays, I surmised.

Made no difference to me.

I was glad she said something.

I never backed down from a little stiff competition.

Or a lot of it.

"What did you say to him?" I asked.

"Something to the effect of how amazing you are, and then something like—guess we'll see who solves the Holliday case first. I had no idea Blackwell and Foley weren't aware you're a private detective now, or that you'd decided to take on murder cases. I'm sorry. I feel so bad."

I laughed. "Don't be. They were going to find out soon enough. I'm glad it's out in the open."

"You know they're going to be all over you about this now, right?"

I did.

To expect anything less wasn't realistic.

The bartender set two martinis down in front of us—a lemon drop martini for Simone and a dirty martini for me. Simone raised her glass, clanked hers against mine, and said, "Oh, and one more thing ... I want in!"

"In?"

"This new detective agency you're starting up with Hunter."

"Detective Agency ... what are you ... hang on a second. I haven't hired her yet. Hell, I don't even know what *I'm* doing yet. It's just getting off the ground. Besides, you already have a job."

"Forensic anthropology doesn't have to be a full-time job, and I'm not suggesting I quit. I love working at the lab with Silas. I just get the feeling Blackwell might find a way to squeeze me out."

"What makes you think that?"

"We have history. Feels like a lifetime ago when I worked as a detective in his department. He's the reason why I switched careers, as you know. And look at me, Gigi. I'm not white. I'm not a yes-man, and I don't suck up to him. I don't fit into his world, not even a little bit."

Anger rose inside me. I pushed it down.

Unlike the meek, mild Hunter, Simone could fight her own battle, and she'd have no problem doing it.

Simone nudged me. "Hey, are you all right?"

"Just went down Blackwell memory lane for a minute. I'm back."

"Look, all I want is to be a part of whatever it is you're doing," she said. "Even if it's a small part. We're a trio of strong, talented women, all former detectives. Maybe you don't think you need us, but together, I believe we'd make a great team."

"I agree. Still, I need to think about it."

"I'm sure you do. I'm not going anywhere."

I reached for my martini, and my phone buzzed. I pulled it out of my pocket and answered.

"Detective Germaine?" a shaky female voice said.

"Yeah, who's this?"

"Greer Holliday."

"I was going to call you in the morning with an update. Were you aware your sister and Trevor Armstrong were seeing each other again? According to him—"

"Please, I need you to listen."

I listened, and what I heard was panic in her voice.

Something was wrong.

"Greer, are you all right?'

"I'm … no. I just sat down to dinner with Cooper, and the doorbell rang. I answered it, and no one was there. There was a note stuck to the door. A piece of paper with the number 1 on it, just like I saw at my sister's house."

"Give me your address. I'll be right there."

"It's 516 Hallifax …"

Silence.

"Greer? Are you there? Talk to me."

"I-I don't feel so good."

I heard a loud thump, like something, or someone, had just hit the floor. I bolted out of my seat, wrapped my jacket around me, and turned toward Simone. "I'm sorry. I need to go."

10

I rushed to 516 Hallifax Street, my mind racing over my phone call with Greer. Since leaving the bar, I'd called her half a dozen times. No answer. And now I needed to call to someone else—someone I'd been hoping to avoid.

The phone rang several times before it was answered with a harsh, "Yeah? What is it?"

"Chief Blackwell? This is Georgiana Germaine."

"No kidding. Why are you calling? What do you want?"

"I was hired by Greer Holliday to look into the death of her sister, as I'm sure you've heard."

"What of it?" he grunted.

"She just called me, and I think something's wrong. I'm headed to her place to check things out and thought I'd give you a heads up."

"*Why* do you think something's wrong?"

I relayed the brief conversation I'd had with Greer.

He yawned—loud and clear—and said, "You're being rather impulsive, don't you think? Overreacting, if you ask me. I'm sure it's nothing. Her cell phone could have lost charge. Women forget to charge their cell phones all the time."

Women.

I guess men were immune to such nonsense.

It didn't matter what he'd said. He was agitated. I could hear it in his voice. He knew the note with the number 1 stuck to Greer's door was not an accident, nor was it impulsive of me to assume she was in imminent danger. Even so, he'd tried to play it off, making me regret my decision to call him.

"Look, I know you don't like me, and that's fine," I said. "But this call isn't about me. It's about her, and I'm telling you, something's not right. You know it isn't."

There was a long pause, followed by, "From now on, call Foley, not me. Any working relationship we had is over."

The line went dead.

I arrived at Greer's place five minutes later. Her door was ajar several inches and judging by the charred smell wafting through the air, something was burning. I sprinted inside, scanning the house for its occupants.

"Greer? Cooper? Anyone?"

No Greer.

No Cooper.

I yelled her name.

I yelled his name.

Still nothing.

In the kitchen, I found scorched brownies in a pan in the oven. Assuming the oven was still on, I went to turn it off and noticed someone had already done it.

Why turn the stove off and leave the brownies to burn?

Curious.

Two plates of uneaten pasta were on the kitchen table. A half-full glass of red wine rested next to the stove as if Greer had been sipping it while she prepared dinner. The wine bottle wasn't far away.

Where was she?

Where was Cooper?

I entered the hallway, pushing doors open along the way, calling out to Greer as I poked my head inside each room. I reached the master suite and stepped inside, slapping a hand against my lips as I made a harsh discovery. Greer was lying in the center of the bed, her eyes closed. Her hands were crossed over her heart in the same ritualistic pose seen at Pippa's crime scene. A lock of hair was missing, and she was facing a note with the number 1 written on it, which was affixed to her dresser drawer.

I walked over and felt for a pulse, even though I knew it was pointless.

All it took was one look, and I knew she was dead.

I jerked my cell phone out of my pocket and dialed 9-1-1, gave specific details, and then ended the call. My thoughts shifted to Cooper. Was he still here, in the house somewhere? Or had he been taken this time?

A second scan of the house yielded nothing, no sign of him.

I buried my face in my hands, allowing the disappointment I felt to wash over me. Not only was I nowhere near solving Pippa's case, but now Greer was also dead. Cooper was missing. My usual self-confidence slipped. My first case as a private eye was a mess, a disaster of colossal proportions.

As I indulged in a pity party for one, I heard a distinct sound—sniffling—coming from inside one of the kitchen cabinets. I rushed over, bent down, and flung the door open, my eyes brimming with tears at the scene in front of me. There, curled into a ball on the bottom shelf, I found a terrified, beautiful little boy.

11

Hey, bud. Are you Cooper?" I asked.

He blinked at me but didn't utter a word.

"It's okay," I said. "I'm Georgiana, Aunt Greer's friend."

He wrapped his arms tighter around his legs and buried his head in his chest.

"I understand," I said. "You're scared. I'd be scared too. You can come out if you want. It's safe."

He shook his head.

"All right. Just stay there for now. It'll be okay. I'm going to make a phone call."

Against my better judgment, I dialed the one number I had in connection with Pippa, hoping to get some answers.

The call was answered, and I wasted no time getting to the point.

"Where are you right now?" I asked.

"Who is this?" Trevor asked.

"Detective Germaine. *Where* are you?"

"At the restaurant, closing up for the evening."

"Can you prove it?"

"Why should I?"

"It's important."

"How do you expect me to prove it?"

I ended the call and dialed the restaurant's number. A man answered and then passed the phone to Trevor, who sounded a lot more frustrated this time around.

"Tell me what this is all about or I'm hanging up," he said.

"Where's your daughter tonight?"

"I don't know. I'm her father, not her watchdog. I'm hanging up now."

"Wait. Please. I shouldn't be telling you this, but since it will be all over the news by morning anyway ... Greer Holliday is dead."

"What? When?"

"Tonight."

"I can assure you I've been at the restaurant for the last three hours. Anyone on my staff can confirm that. Where's Cooper? Is he okay?"

"He's with me, and he's the reason I'm calling," I said. "What family did Pippa have other than her sister? Anyone close by?"

"Her parents live in Africa. Zambia, I believe. They're doctors. When they retired, they moved there to volunteer. None of her other relatives live close by."

"What about friends?"

"Oh, yes. Alli Kane. They went to school together. She and Pippa were close. She's also Cooper's godmother. She doesn't live far. She's over in Paso Robles."

"Alli's his godmother, but she doesn't have any *legal* rights to him, does she?"

"Pippa had a will. From what I understand, Alli was supposed to raise Cooper in the event of Pippa's death, not Greer."

"Then why was he living with Greer?"

"When I spoke to Alli at Pippa's funeral, she said Greer took

Cooper to her place as soon as she found out Pippa had died. Alli brought up the will, and Greer said Alli would have to fight her in court to get custody."

"Do you have Alli's number?"

"Think so. We got together as couples a few times. Hang on."

I waited.

"Found it," he said.

He gave me the number, and I ended the call.

I walked back to the cupboard and got on my knees, hoping if I was eye level, I'd be less intimidating.

"Hey, buddy," I said. "Do you know Alli, your mom's friend?"

His eyes flickered. He recognized the name.

"I want Alli," he sobbed.

"Okay, honey. I'll call her. You can even talk to her on the phone if you want. Can you come out of the cupboard for me? We can call her together."

He thought about it and stared at me for a long while before he decided to crawl on out. We placed a call to Alli, and within a few minutes, she was in her car and on her way. Since the house was now a crime scene, I told her to head to the police department and wait for me there.

The front door opened, and I leaned over, peering into the living room. I was expecting the paramedics. Instead, a man entered the house. I pushed Cooper behind me and told him to stay close.

I grabbed my gun, readied it, and waited.

The man rounded the corner, looked at me, and reached for his own gun.

"Uh-uh," I said, shaking my head. "Don't even think about it."

"Put the gun down," he said.

"Who are you? Why are you here?"

"Who are *you*? Why are *you* here?"

His attention shifted from me to Cooper. "Hey there, kiddo. What's your name?"

I waved my weapon at the man. "Don't speak to him. Speak to me."

"You know, pulling a gun on me isn't a good idea."

"You're right. It's a great one."

He took a step toward me.

"Don't," I said. "Move any closer, and I will shoot you."

"Shoot me? For what? Standing too close to you?"

He tossed his head back and laughed.

"It's not funny," I said. "Nothing about this is funny. Answer my question. Who are you?"

"Ladies first."

Asshole of the first degree.

Fine.

"Detective Georgiana Germaine. Your turn."

"You do mean *former* detective, right? Do try to keep up with the turn of events."

I connected the dots as to who he was and why he was there. "Ah, I know who you are."

"And who am I?"

"Well now, let's see … so far, you act like Blackwell. You look a bit like him too, if he were twenty years younger and had a hideous haircut."

"Ouch. He warned me about your, ehh, how do I put this? Your fiery temperament and lack of tact."

Fiery?

He didn't know the half of it.

"This isn't the way I wanted us to meet, Detective Foley," I said. "But here we are."

He glanced around. "What? No mafia boyfriend joining you today to offer protection?"

"Do I look like I need protecting?"

"You look like you need therapy."

It wasn't the first time it had been suggested, and it wouldn't be the last.

"Trust me," I said. "I've come a long way from the woman I was a couple of years ago. Be grateful you're not meeting *her* today, though I should warn you. She does poke her head in from time to time."

"Noted."

The sound of screaming sirens were heard pulling up outside.

I holstered my gun as the paramedics filed in.

Foley turned toward them—planning to bark orders, no doubt—but the female paramedic who walked in first looked past him and grinned at me.

She raced over, wrapping her arms around me. "Georgiana! We've missed you!"

"I've missed you too."

"Where are we headed?"

"Back bedroom."

She nodded, looked at the rest of her crew, and said, "Back bedroom, boys. Let's go."

She breezed past Foley like he wasn't there, which I had to admit was the highlight of my day. He cursed under his breath and took out his phone, I guessed to call Blackwell. I took mine out too. I had another, more pressing call to make, and it couldn't wait a moment longer.

12

There was a good chance Cooper had witnessed his aunt's murder. Even if he hadn't, he'd been in the house when it happened. Foley and Blackwell would be tenacious about visiting with him. I understood. As a detective, I was interested in what he'd seen or heard too. But looking at him now, he was in shock. In a short period of time, he'd lost his mother and his aunt, and he was in no condition to be grilled by anyone right now.

Silas entered the house, his eyes wide when he saw me in the kitchen. He tipped his head to the side, and I took Cooper's hand and led him into the living room. I turned on the television, found a cartoon for him to watch, then joined Silas by the fireplace.

"Hey, so what happened?" Silas whispered. "Anything I should know?"

"The victim, Greer Holliday, was Pippa's sister, the woman who hired me."

He ran a hand through his hair. "Oh, wow. Explains why you're here, then."

"Greer called me tonight."

"What time?"

"Just before seven."

"What did you talk about?"

"She said she didn't feel good. I was about to ask why, and then I heard a loud crashing sound, like she fell. I came straight over. By the time I arrived, she was already dead."

"How long did it take you to get here?"

"I checked the time when I left and again when I reached the house. Twenty-two minutes. I think the killer was here, in the house, when she called me. If I'm right, he still took the time to stage the body. Other than Pippa being found by the pool and Greer being found in her bed, the staging was the same—the note, arms crossed over her chest, hair missing."

"What are you thinking?"

"She either found out something about Pippa's murder and became a target as a result, or she was an intended target, just like her sister. And then there's Cooper. He was in the house at the time of both murders, and each time, he was spared. Why? Was it because he's an innocent child? Or is there some other reason? If he's a potential witness, why would the killer leave him here?"

"Huh. He wasn't the target, and he's so young. Maybe that's why he was spared. Who knows? I'm just glad the little guy is alive."

"Me too."

I glanced over at Cooper. He was young, too young to experience so much heartbreak in such a short amount of time. What damage had already been done—damage he'd be saddled with for the remainder of his life? I wanted to wave a magic wand over his head and send him back to the past, to a place where his mother and aunt were still alive and life wasn't a series of tragedies.

"Hey, umm, when you dust for prints, make sure to get the stove, the knobs, and everything around it," I said.

"Why single out the stove?"

"I found a batch of burnt brownies in the oven when I first got here, but the stove had been turned off. I doubt the kid did it. He couldn't reach the knobs unless he used a chair."

"I'll make sure we go over the entire thing." Silas patted me on the shoulder. "What now? Will you keep going with the investigation even though your client's dead?"

"You've known me a long time," I said. "What do you think? Besides, she paid me. But even if she hadn't, I wouldn't walk away—not now. Cooper deserves justice, and I intend to make sure he gets it."

Silas was no longer listening. He was watching a shadow move along the wall. "I, uhh … I *think* someone's eavesdropping on our conversation, or trying to, anyway."

He was right.

Our meddler was meddling a little too close.

Foley rounded the corner and headed straight for us.

"You're here to do a job, Silas," Foley said. "Not to waste time fraternizing with Miss Germaine. If you have anything to say, anything to report, you report it to me. Got it?"

Silas mumbled a quick "right, sure," and then darted down the hallway toward the master bedroom.

Foley bent down on one knee and reached for Cooper's hand.

Cooper recoiled.

"Hey, Cooper. My name is Detective Foley, and I need to take you for a ride. Don't worry. You're safe with me. If you want, we can even stop off at McDonald's along the way and get you a Happy Meal. Would you like that?"

"You're not taking him anywhere," I said.

"This isn't your business any longer. Your client is dead."

"Whether she's alive or not, she hired me to do a job. It's my business as long as I say it is."

"Blackwell wants to speak to the boy."

"I'm sure he does, but in my opinion, the boy's not ready."

"It's not for you to decide."

"Funny, because I already have."

I joined Cooper on the sofa, resting a protective arm in front of him.

Foley tapped his foot, seeming to contemplate what to do next. "Oh, come on, Germaine. You have no right stopping me from doing my job. You of all people know that."

The front door opened, and in walked Tiffany Wheeler, the mayor's daughter and an old schoolmate of mine. Foley looked her up and down, confused about who she was and why she was here.

"Foley, I'd like to introduce you to Tiffany Wheeler," I said. "She's a lawyer, and as of thirty minutes ago, she represents Cooper Holliday and Alli Kane, his legal guardian."

"Legal guardian? Who's Alli Kane?"

"She's a friend of Pippa Holliday."

He remained still and silent a moment as if he were trying to wrap his head around the coup I'd just pulled off.

"Here's what's going to happen now," I said. "We'll take Cooper to the department where Alli Kane is waiting. I'll leave it to Alli and Tiffany to assess whether Blackwell or you get the chance to talk to Cooper tonight."

Tiffany nodded.

I scooped Cooper into my arms, glancing back at Foley as I walked out the front door. "And Foley ... do try to keep up with the turn of events."

13

An hour later, after going multiple rounds with Blackwell, Tiffany managed to convince him to hold off on questioning Cooper. The boy needed time. How much, we couldn't be sure, but tonight was not the night he'd be talking. Upon first glimpse of Alli walking his way, Cooper had run into her open arms, tears flowing as he buried his head in her chest. At long last, he'd found his security blanket, the place where he felt safe.

After a long, tiresome day, I arrived home to an overenthusiastic Luka, who ran circles around my feet, as he waited for me to reach down and give him some pats. It seemed my security blanket had found me too.

"I know, buddy. I missed you just as much as you missed me."

Giovanni was in the living room wearing a black cashmere robe. His damp, black hair had been slicked back, and he held a pencil in one hand, staring through reading glasses as he worked a crossword puzzle.

He raised a finger in the air and said, "Mrs. Danvers is the creepy housekeeper in which classic novel? Seven letters."

"*Rebecca.*"

He penciled in the answer and looked up. "I believe you're right."

I winked and said, "Of course I am."

He put the puzzle book down and patted the empty space next to him. "You must be tired."

I leaned back on the sofa and rested my head against his shoulder. "I am. I feel like my internal battery has gone flat and is unable to accept any and all future charges."

"I figured as much. When you called to say you were on your way home, I ran you a bath. Go soak for a while. You'll feel better."

"You're not joining me?"

"I can. I thought you'd enjoy some time to yourself."

"I'd enjoy some time together. Besides, I want to run something by you."

"All right. Bath time it is. I'll pour you a glass of wine and see you in five."

He kissed me on the forehead and headed toward the kitchen with Luka in tow, no doubt hopeful he'd soon be the recipient of a doggie treat upon arrival.

I sunk into the luxury of bubbles and warmth, trying my best to allow all my current worries to evaporate like the steam vanishing into the air above me.

Giovanni walked in carrying two glasses of wine. He set one next to me, and then stepped into the tub on the other side.

"You're too far away," I said. "I swear, this thing could hold ten people."

He scooted closer and laughed. "Ten people, and it would become a much different kind of party."

I shook my head and reached for my wine.

"What's on your mind?" he asked.

"When I left the department to start my own PI business, I figured I'd be working alone. Simone and Hunter have suggested we go into business together. Simone would do it on the side. Hunter sees it as more of full-time career where she'd work a variety of different cases."

"And what do you think about the proposition?"

"It's something I've never thought about, not until Hunter quit her job. I want to take high-profile cases like the one I'm working now. The grittier the better."

"You mean *the riskier the better*, don't you?"

"Sometimes I think you'd lock me inside a glass box if you could."

"I have no desire to hold you back. At the same time, I want you to be safe."

"I *am* safe."

"Today. What about tomorrow? With you, there will always be a next time. Taking on murder cases yourself involves more risk. You're impulsive. You put yourself in dangerous situations without giving it much thought."

I wanted to tell him he was wrong.

We both knew he wasn't.

I splashed a handful of water his direction and said, "Are you suggesting if I teamed up with Simone and Hunter, you'd feel better?"

"I'm suggesting a compromise."

I didn't follow.

"What kind of compromise?" I asked.

He dipped his hands into the water and ran them across his face. Whatever he needed to say, he seemed concerned about my reaction to it.

"Whatever it is, just tell me," I said.

"All right. I will. I'd like you to consider allowing Peppe to accompany you on your high-risk cases."

"Why?"

"Because I can't always be here, and you have a knack for getting yourself into trouble."

"I don't need a shadow looking over my shoulder all the time. Besides, Peppe's a … you know …"

Giovanni narrowed his eyes. "He's a what?"

Gangster.

Through and through.

He may have slowed down some—he'd just rounded the corner into his sixties—but I imagined his younger days were filled with the kind of stories I never wanted to hear about.

"He's no different than I am," Giovanni said. "You chose to be with me, chose to move in together, knowing the man I am now and the one I was in the past. You cannot have it both ways, cara mia. You cannot accept one side of me without accepting the other."

"You said it's different now, that you've stepped away from the family business."

"Stepped away doesn't mean stepped out. I'll never be out, not all the way. I'd do anything for my family. You'd do the same for yours too."

He was right.

I would.

But my family didn't require the same sacrifice his did.

Over the last two years, we'd had several conversations similar to the one we were having now. Except tonight, I was seeing the picture in its entirety for the first time. Seeing all of *him* for the first time. Up to now, I'd veiled myself, told myself the man in front of me, the man I knew, was the only one that existed.

In ways, I'd lied to myself.

And now, I wasn't sure how I felt about it.

14

In my dream, I was standing in a bright-white room. Opposite me, two young girls with wavy blond hair, dressed in long, red dresses stood next to each other. They were holding hands. The girl on the left had the number 1 written in red ink in the center of her forehead. The girl on the right didn't.

The girl with the number on her forehead let go of the other girl's hand. She whispered something into her ear, and they both started giggling. Then they started chasing each other around the room.

They circled around me a few times, behaving as if I weren't there, and then they stopped. The girl with the number on her forehead high-fived the other, and then she turned to me, pointing at the opposite side of the room. I followed her finger and noticed a black door had appeared, a door that wasn't there before.

Both girls ran toward it.

When the girl with the number on her forehead reached the door, she turned and waved me over. She opened the door, stuck her head through, and yelled something I couldn't make out. Even though she was standing right in front of me, it was like she was talking inside a fishbowl.

The other girl slammed the door before I could see what was on the other side and turned around. They began whispering again and then they leaned against the door, putting all their weight against it. The girls clasped hands as someone began pounding on the opposite side of the door.

I stood in front of them and said, "Open it. I want to see who's behind the door."

In unison, they shook their heads.

"You're trying to show me something, aren't you? Why not let me see what you're hiding?"

The girl with the number on her forehead tugged on the sleeve of my shirt and said, "Wanna know a secret? I'm dead."

I pointed at the other girl. "Is *she* dead too?"

"No. Not yet."

"What's behind the door?"

"It's not a what, silly. It's a *who*."

The girl without the number on her head said, "Do you like riddles?"

"Sometimes," I said. "Do you know any?"

"I know one."

"Tell it to me."

"A bad lady kidnapped lots of women. She gave each woman two cookies and a glass of water. She told each of them to eat one cookie and then warned them that one of the cookies was poisonous. The other was not. Whichever cookie the women did not eat, the bad lady ate. All the women chose the poisonous cookie, and they all died. How did they all choose the poisonous cookie?"

"I don't know. How?"

"The poison wasn't in the cookies. It was in the water."

As soon as she said the word *water*, the room collapsed, submerging us all underwater. I swam around, looking for the girls. They were gone. Floating around me were hundreds of pieces of paper, all inked with the number 1.

My eyes flashed open, and I woke from my dream.

15

When visiting prison, apparel choice mattered a lot more than one would think. Nothing too tight, too short, too form-fitting, too revealing. Nothing strapless or transparent. Nothing to cause a stir. Nothing to send the wrong message. Nothing to invite unwanted attention. No hats. No gloves. And *no* shower shoes.

When I'd dressed earlier that morning, standing in front of the mirror as I tried multiple options to see which outfit worked best, three specific words came to mind.

Conservative.

Modest.

Appropriate.

These were just a few of the requirements for anyone wishing to access a golden ticket to the women's state prison. Today, I'd ditched my usual vintage style and opted for a more subdued look. A simple white shirt, black bottoms, and flats, and I'd pinned my violet-colored, shoulder-length hair back into a bun.

As I headed out of the house, I thought about the dream I'd

had the night before. It was strange, and yet I was certain it was significant in a way I'd not yet realized but soon would. The girl with the number 1 on her forehead was the key to the old case and the new. There was a reason Wolfe left one of her alleged murders to the imagination. Figure that out, and maybe I'd catch my killer.

On my way to the prison, I called Harvey, and we discussed what he recalled about the investigation. Though it had been decades since he and my father had locked Wolfe away, he still retained a lot of important details about the case, including the autopsies of the victims, the crime scenes, and conversations he'd had with Wolfe prior to her trial date. Before we ended the call, he told me to remember the training I'd received about dealing with a person in this situation, suggesting I might even try interviewing her in a low-light setting to create a more informal, stress-free environment.

It wasn't a bad idea.

But I doubted I'd be given the option to control the interview environment.

"You're not there to interrogate her," he'd said. "Your job is to make her feel relaxed enough that she's willing to keep talking. She's intelligent, smarter than most. Expect her to ask you about yourself, your life, personal details even. Tell her as much as you can, whether she asks or she doesn't. It will build trust between the two of you. She's not going anywhere. She'll die in that prison, so you won't do yourself any favors by holding back."

This sage advice had been offered to me because he knew I needed it. I tended to be impulsive, even brash at times. This was the perfect opportunity to practice a little restraint—or a lot of it—in order to get what I wanted.

I arrived at the prison, showed my ID, signed in, was searched top to bottom and then told what to do and what not to do during my time with Wolfe. I was escorted to a room where I chatted with Warden Jackson for a while, going over my main areas of focus. Jackson then admitted something I didn't know—a few months earlier Wolfe had been interviewed by a woman from *Serial Crime Magazine*. The article had been published the previous month. I made a mental note to read it once the interview with Wolfe was over.

Warden Jackson exited the room, and I waited, and waited, and then waited some more. I passed the time thinking about what I knew about Wolfe. She'd been adopted by loving parents at six months of age. Upon her arrival, they learned her birth parents had named her Atticus. An unusual name, which had been the birth father's idea. He wanted a boy. He got a girl, and his interest in the relationship soured. He walked out on his teenage girlfriend, saying he'd never wanted to be a parent in the first place.

Atticus' mother held out a bit longer, keeping the newborn for several months before she decided raising a baby was too hard. She was young, broke, and desperate to live a life free of the shackles that came with teen parenthood. When Atticus' new parents came into the picture, they chose to honor the name she'd been given, but calling her "Addy" for short.

Atticus "Addy" Wolfe was raised in a privileged household in a privileged neighborhood with privileged friends. She was smart, with a genius level IQ of 140. By the time she was an adult, she knew how to charm and manipulate, how to bend others to her will, and how to crawl inside a person's mind and stay there.

At age twenty-eight, Wolfe killed for the first time. Jill Jacobsen was a twenty-four-year-old cashier working at one of the local grocery stores Wolfe frequented. Wolfe wouldn't commit murder again for another two years. Nikki Daley, her second victim, was a waitress who worked in a diner less than five miles from Wolfe's residence. After Jill and Nikki, the murders became more frequent. Two each year for the next three years.

All women.

All poisoned.

All staged.

She kept souvenirs of her kills in the form of a lock of hair, which she'd clipped from each victim, bagged, and stored in a container in her freezer for safe keeping.

Just when she thought she was above ever getting caught, she slipped up. Assuming her ninth was dead, Wolfe posed her in the same way she'd posed the others, crossing Sarah Peterson's hands over her heart, tilting her head to the side, and chopping off a thick lock of hair.

Except Sarah Peterson *wasn't* dead when Wolfe fled the scene.

She was *almost* dead.

Moments later, Sarah's boyfriend entered the house to find his girlfriend barely clinging to life. She'd been administered the poison, in a similar dosage as had been given to Wolfe's other victims, but somehow, Sarah managed to survive. One week later, Sarah named her murderer—Addy Wolfe—a woman she'd befriended just two weeks earlier in a café on Main Street.

At the trial, Wolfe confessed to nine murders, even though there had only been eight. When asked to explain, she just grinned and said, "Wouldn't *you* like to know?"

Everyone assumed Wolfe couldn't bring herself to admit she'd botched her ninth murder, the reason she confessed to nine murders instead of eight.

Sentenced to life without the possibility of parole, she fell into oblivion, a person few discussed and even fewer remembered. It seemed to me she'd almost been forgotten because of how quiet she'd been about the murders over the years. She never spoke about why she'd committed them, how she chose her victims, or about the catalyst that drove her to kill in the first place. Hard-core criminologists had their theories, of course, but without Wolfe to confirm them, none had ever been proven.

There were two main commonalities in Wolfe's victims:

1. They were all women.
2. Wolfe befriended each of them before they died, most knowing her for a brief period of two to four weeks.

Now, it seemed, Wolfe had opened up at long last, agreeing to be interviewed—first by a woman from a magazine, and now by me.

What I wanted to know was … *why?*

Why the change of heart?

Why now?

As I pondered this question, the door opened, and Atticus Wolfe was escorted to the table by two armed guards. For a woman of seventy, she looked good. Fit. Competent. Strong, yet feminine. Her long, gray hair was vibrant and shiny, her complexion milky and smooth, like she was wearing makeup even though she wasn't. She lowered herself into the seat and thanked the guards. Then she locked eyes on me, flashing me a wry grin as she said, "It took you long enough."

16

Were you expecting me sooner?" I asked.

"You, or someone like you. No matter. How's your father?"

She was toying with me, right out of the gate.

She knew about my father.

Everyone did.

Perhaps it was a test, and she wanted to see if my cage would rattle. She was about to learn it seldom did.

"My father is dead," I said. "But you know that already."

"I meant your *other* father. Haven't seen Harvey since ... oh, let's see now. Must have been around the 1980s when I was left to rot in this place. How is the old softie?"

"Retired."

"Retired, eh? Sounds boring. And you? You stepped up after your father died, followed in his footsteps, just like he said you would."

It seemed, back in the day, my father had discussed me with a convicted felon.

Fantastic.

What else did she know?

"I had many conversations with your father before I was convicted, and a few after," she continued. "Abe never called you by name. He called you G. Yesterday I learned your name is Georgiana Germaine. The shoe fits, does it not?"

What "fit" was Harvey's comment about Wolfe's intelligence. She'd wasted no time taking the reins, letting me know she believed she could bend and shift the conversation at will.

"What else did my father talk to you about?" I asked.

"Being a father. He loved it. Loved you and your siblings. The lot of you mattered to him more than anything else in life, I'd say."

"He was a great man. I miss him."

"And Harvey ... is *he* a great man too?"

"He's a great everything."

She cocked her head to the side. "What a surprise. I always found him somewhat bland, a little slow to crack the whip, if you know what I mean. Then again, he wasted no time marrying your mother after your father passed. Abe wasn't even cold in his grave yet. Must have been hard on you and your siblings."

After my father's death, Harvey spent all his free time by our side, holding our hands as we navigated our way through the darkest days of our lives. It was during this time that he bonded with my mother.

Mom mourned the husband she'd adored.

Harvey mourned the loss of a fellow detective and best friend.

Together, they found comfort, a way to navigate through tragedy and loss.

The night they sat us kids down, admitting their love for one another, it wasn't as difficult for us to take as they assumed it would be. We'd seen the glances they'd exchanged in previous months, Harvey's hand resting on my mother's arm. There had been extra-long embraces as he left our house to head home each night. In my opinion, we were aware of their feelings before they were.

"You seem to know a lot about my family," I said.

"Guess you could say I'm well liked around this place. If I want information, there's always a way to find it."

Good to know.

"You agreed to be interviewed for a magazine not too long ago," I said. "I didn't think you gave interviews."

Her lips curved into a slight grin. "I've had multiple requests to be interviewed over the years. Dozens, in fact. Half a dozen wanted to turn my life into a book, or a true-crime program. Donna Reagan is the first person I've agreed to speak to in all the time I've been incarcerated."

"Why her? Why now?"

"I'm aging. It's time."

I didn't believe her.

There must have been another reason, something other than waking up one day and having an epiphany that this was the right time to start talking. For now, I decided not to push. I didn't want to run the risk of angering her and having our visit cut short.

She leaned in closer. "Have you read it—*my* article?"

"I will later today. I look forward to it."

The fact I knew about the article and hadn't read it yet displeased her.

It showed on her face.

Strike one.

"I could recite it word for word, but I won't spoil it for you," she said. "Why are you here, Germaine? Why come to see me today? Best get right to it."

I wasn't ready to talk about the case just yet.

First, I had other questions.

I wanted to get to know her, who she was and is, and what made her do what she did. In doing so, I'd create a more accurate profile of Pippa and Greer's murderer.

"I'd like to know more about your childhood," I said.

"What about it?"

"You were adopted as a baby. Did you like your adoptive parents? Your siblings?"

"If you're asking me to compare my childhood to any other's childhood, I wouldn't know what to say. Was it average, good, great? It was all those things. My parents were parents. They did the best they could. They tried. My siblings were the same. Tell me about yours."

"You already know about my siblings."

"Are you close?"

"I consider them friends, though we're not as close as we could be."

"Why not?"

"Too busy, I guess. It's not their fault. It's mine."

"In what way?"

I knew the answer. I just didn't want to give it.

Still, I felt the need to give her something.

"I don't share as much of myself as I could with my siblings. Sometimes I catch myself holding back, and not just with them either. I'm the same way with most people."

She raised a brow, nodding like she understood the feeling. "Do you believe if you let them see the real you—the dark, twisted, tainted sides of yourself, the sides you hate about yourself—they would see you in a different way? Would they not love you as much? Or do you fear they wouldn't love you at all?"

I found myself struggling to open up about myself, like Harvey had suggested, for the sake of my own agenda. She knew of my agenda, too. I was sure of it. And yet, the way her eyes flickered with each admission I made told me she was as curious about my backstory as I was about hers. It was in my best interest to keep it that way.

"I tell myself what others think of me doesn't matter," I said. "I do care, I suppose, a lot more than I should at times. Guess it's why I get close to some people, but never *too* close. What about you? Are you close to anyone?"

"As close as one can be in this hamster cage." She tapped her finger to the table. "I had a good relationship with my brother, Daniel. I could tell him anything, no matter how hard it was for him to hear, and he'd still come see me. It didn't matter what I'd done. He supported me in a way most never would."

She'd spoken of Daniel in the past tense.

Was he ... *dead?*

I chided myself for not knowing the answer.

"Did something happen to your brother?" I asked.

She huffed an irritated, "For a detective, you sure don't do a great deal of detecting, do you?"

Strike two.

"I'm knowledgeable about your past. I apologize for not knowing more about the present. You're right. I should know more than I do."

"Daniel never met a cigarette he didn't like. He died of lung cancer. Five months ago. Started smoking when he was thirteen. Shame, you know. I miss seeing him. Miss our conversations. Would you like some advice?"

No, I wouldn't.

Not from you.

"Sure," I said.

"There's something refreshing about sharing every fiber of your being with another person. It's a rush, a feeling you'll never understand until you experience it. Speak your truth, Germaine.

Only then will you see who is there for you and who isn't. Only then will you know how to separate the flowers from the weeds."

It was a strange feeling, being counseled by a serial murderer, even if there was truth in her words. She was a killer, a fact it would be unwise of me to forget.

"Do you have the same relationship with your sister?" I asked.

"Christine? No. She severed all ties the day of my arrest."

"What about Nancy, your other sister? Were the two of you close?"

"She's been gone so long now, it's hard for me to remember. I don't think much about the past. It's gone. What's the point?"

On a warm, summer day, seventeen-year-old Nancy and eighteen-year-old Daniel decided to spend the day waterskiing. Given their parents were out of town for the weekend, they assumed a quick trip to the lake with the family boat wouldn't be noticed. About an hour into the adventure, they hit a series of waves. Daniel, who was behind the wheel, attempted to slow down, but it was too late. He'd been going fast—too fast—and when the waves came crashing in, Nancy shot into the air, tumbling back down to the choppy water below. She sustained multiple head and neck injuries on impact and died minutes later, in the arms of her inconsolable brother.

"What happened to your sister must have been hard for your family," I said. "Daniel, in particular."

"Death happens to us all at some point. Whether we choose to grieve or not doesn't change the inevitable. It doesn't bring anyone back. I expect you understand that more than anyone."

"Grief, for me, is about the loss itself—the fact that I'll wake up each day never being able to touch that person again, talk to them, feel the warmth of their embrace. I grieved all of those things after my father died."

"I'm not speaking about your father."

In that moment, I clued in.

She was speaking about Fallon, my daughter.

"We can talk about whatever you like, but not her," I said.

"She's off-limits."

"If grief is about the loss, why not tell me about it?"

"I don't like talking about her."

"Is it because you can't touch her, talk to her, feel her warmth as you say? Or is it because of the guilt you've shackled yourself with because *you* know you're the one who's responsible for her death?"

"Stop it."

"Don't waste time fretting over your daughter or what you did or didn't do the day of the accident. Doesn't matter how it happened or why. Doesn't matter if the gate to the pool came unlatched while you stepped into the house for a moment. She's dead. You're alive. That's it."

It was a rare instance when I didn't know what to say, when I lacked an irreverent comeback to such a comment. She knew more about me than I knew about her. As such, she'd rattled me. And no matter how much I told myself I could handle visiting with her, that I was prepared for her and this conversation, there was one upper hand here, and it wasn't mine.

I stood. "I just, uh, need a minute. Can I ... can we, take five?"

She tipped her head back and laughed. "Sixteen minutes."

"What?"

"Sixteen minutes was all it took to break you. If you expect me to talk to you, I expect *you* to show me who you are—who you *really* are—not this shell of a person pussyfooting around like a nervous puppy cowering in the corner."

"I'm not cowering."

"Now you're lying to me. Or you're lying to yourself. I gave you a shot, one shot to dig your claws in, and you won't even take it. What a disappointment you are." She turned to the guard standing to her left. "Tom, we're done here."

Strike three, Gigi.

You're out.

17

As the guards moved to Wolfe's side, preparing to escort her back to her cell block, I pulled my head out and started playing the game—on *my* terms this time.

"You've given your opinion about me," I said. "Now I'll give you my opinion about you."

Wolfe made eyes with one of the guards and said, "Well, well. The investigator knows how to speak for herself after all. What do you think, Tom? Should I allow her a few more minutes of my precious time, or shall we tell her to screw off and be done with it?"

Tom looked at her and then at me like he wished he was anywhere else right then. "I mean, I don't know. Up to you, I guess. You've still got time."

"Decisions, decisions." She paused a moment longer for dramatic effect and then returned to the table. "Are you going to come at me now, the way you've wanted to ever since you arrived? Then do it. Let's see if you have what it takes to live up to your father's name."

This is what she'd wanted all along—to spar, go toe to toe, wit to wit. As a former captain of the debate team in my youth, I lived for a delicious verbal exchange. After Wolfe's dig about my daughter, I was ready to step up to the podium.

"When your brother died, you had no one left to talk to," I said. "No one like *him*. No one to listen to what you had to say. No one to care. No one besides him ever gave a damn about you except your husband, and he committed suicide. Your sister wrote you off when you went to prison, just like your parents, who came to see you once but never again."

"My parents were ashamed of me, ashamed of who I'd become. My mother cried the entire visit. My father tried to reason with me. He couldn't understand how any child of his could turn out the way I did."

"I bet it made you feel irrelevant and misunderstood. They all turned their back on you. Then you lost Daniel, and you decided it was time for a change. Time to let the world know what a force you once were, so you'd never be irrelevant again."

She stared at me.

I stared back.

She opened her mouth and then closed it, narrowed her eyes, and then licked her lips.

"You know what's great about being locked up all this time? After a while, people forget how dangerous I was once upon a time. They see me now as the woman who stands before them today. They see someone old, someone they assume doesn't know how to fight and would choose not to if given the choice. And they relax. A little at first. Then more. Then more, until no one is paying enough attention to anything that's going on around me. They stop poring over my letters, stop scrutinizing every move I make. And that, Germaine, is when the fun begins."

Now we were getting somewhere.

"Is that why you allowed Donna Reagan to interview you?" I asked.

"I've amassed an eclectic collection of fans over the years. I've had marriage proposals. I've received love letters, hate letters. So many people in the world with nothing to do, hoping to connect. I can't give them connection. Even if I was capable, I wouldn't. But answers … answers are something I can give."

"Answers like what motivated you to murder in the first place?"

"People are odd creatures, aren't they? Most living in their quiet, law-abiding bubble as they fall asleep to murder documentaries playing on the television each night." She snorted a laugh. "And they say *I'm* the evil one."

She had a twisted sense of self, which fed into my next topic of conversation.

"I believe you have a copycat," I said. "Someone staging victims just like you did."

"I'm aware of the Holliday sisters. They're the reason you're here today. You didn't come for me. You came for yourself, to learn from me, hoping I will help you find the one person you cannot."

"Not cannot—*have not*. Yet. I will."

"Ahh, yes. You're prolific at finding murderers, aren't you? Every assignment you've been given, you've never failed to find your man."

"Why do you think someone has decided to replicate your crime scenes?"

"My article must have been even more inspiring than I realized."

Inspiring?

Even without reading it, I could think of a lot of other choice words.

"Were you looking for someone to pick up where you left off?" I asked.

"I was looking to tell my side of the story while I still can. If someone decided to act on what they read, it's on them, not me.

You have two murders, both staged to mimic my own. Though I never targeted sisters."

"Why do you think the killer is targeting sisters now?"

"That's for you to figure out, isn't it?"

"Pippa's murder took place less than three weeks before Greer's did. I believe Pippa's was premeditated. As for Greer, I'm not sure. She may have been targeted like her sister was, or she may have stumbled upon information, and she was killed because of it."

Wolfe pondered my theories for a time. "There are many sides to a hexagon, a shape of equal size that leaves no wasted space."

"Meaning?"

"You're seeing simple possibilities. Easy ones. Life isn't simple. It's messy and filthy, filthier than most allow themselves to believe. Murdering sisters is significant."

Significant how?

"Why did you murder all those innocent women?" I asked. "Your motive wasn't money or sex. Was it jealousy? Revenge?"

Wolfe shook her head, laughing. "I've never understood why people like you always try to group serial killers together like we're all part of a club that shares similarities and secret handshakes. And as for you calling the women whose lives I took 'innocent' ... well, that would suggest they were good people. I would suggest they were not."

"Neither Harvey nor my father ever figured out the motivation behind your murders."

"You seem confident in that."

"I talked to Harvey. He's told me what he knows."

"I'm not referring to Harvey."

"If my father knew something, he wouldn't have kept it from his partner and friend."

"Your father visited me in prison once, not long before his car accident. He said he'd done a lot of thinking after they closed my case. He'd developed his own theories about me—the same theories you're trying to work out now."

"What were they?"

She shook her head. "Oh, no. I'm not here to make it easy for you. I will tell you he shared his assumptions with me, and he was right."

"Then why didn't he tell Harvey or someone at the department?"

"I didn't confirm or deny his suspicions. If I had known he wouldn't be around much longer, maybe I would have. Aside from my brother, the time spent with your father meant the most."

"Why?"

"Abe was intelligent and kind. He saw me. He saw who I am, and he still treated me the same way he treated everyone else."

I believed her.

It was a rare instance when he ever said a harsh word about anyone.

Wolfe leaned toward me. "If you made up a profile on me right now, what would you say? And do me a favor. Include even the most unsavory of details in your assessment."

I considered everything I knew about her up to now. "As a killer, you exhibited predatory behavior, choosing to get to know your victims before you killed them. You lack empathy or remorse for those you've killed. You're charming, but superficial. Intelligent in an obnoxious way. You go out of your way to make sure those you communicate with will never connect with you on your level."

"Good start. What else?"

"There's a reason why you murdered women and not men. It's payback, maybe for the mother who rejected you, though your father did so first."

"My mother, birth or otherwise, had nothing to do with it."

"If it wasn't about her, it was about another woman in your life. A woman who had hurt you. Shall I go on?"

"Someone did. The real question you need to ask yourself now is this: why do some women deserve to die and others do not?"

"None of them *deserved* to die."

"You're missing the point."

"Am I? Saying some women deserve to die and others do not would suggest you were a mission-oriented killer."

"One might say I was doing society a favor."

Tom leaned toward Wolfe and said, "Ten minutes."

"All right, Tom. Can I get some water? My throat's turning into sandpaper with all this talking."

Water.

Water skiing.

Nancy Wolfe's boating accident.

The girls from my dream.

The riddle.

Wolfe's birth mother hadn't hurt her. Her adopted mother hadn't hurt her. Someone else had. Someone who'd made her feel discarded and stupid.

"Where were you the day your sister died?" I asked.

She puckered her lips. "That's the best question you've asked me today."

"Your brother said her death was an accident. The police agreed. Earlier in our conversation, you said your brother always supported you, no matter what you'd done."

"Yes, he did."

"Did he protect you too?"

"Little white lies are necessary from time to time. Ask yourself —who *is* Nancy to me?"

She said *is*, not *was*, which told me everything.

"She's number 1. The first person you killed. *You* were driving the boat that day, not your brother. Did you mean for her to die?"

"I've never murdered anyone by accident."

"Your brother protected you, found a way to cover it up. He even convinced everyone else you weren't there. She was his sister too. Why would he do that for you?"

"It all came down to one thing in the end—which one of us he loved more."

"*You* were driving the boat the day Nancy died, not your brother. Right?"

"Oh my," she said. "What a stern accusation."

"Answer me!"

There was a knock at the door. Tom and the other guard assisted Wolfe out of her chair, and then he handed her the cup of water. She downed the entire thing in one go and turned toward me with a wide grin on her face. "Welcome to your enlightenment party, Germaine. Can't wait to see what happens next."

18

was back in Cambria by late afternoon. On the drive home, I contemplated my next steps. What I *wanted* to do was at odds with what I *needed* to do, and it was the kind of itch that wouldn't go away, no matter how much I scratched it.

I turned into the parking lot of the San Luis Obispo Police Department and pulled to a stop next to Blackwell's shiny red pickup. I sat a moment, tapping my thumb against the steering wheel, rehearsing what I wanted to say in my mind. Before I got the chance to head inside, Blackwell and Foley walked out the front door, too engaged in conversation with one another to notice my presence.

Blackwell smacked Foley on the shoulder, and they burst out laughing.

Then they saw me, and the laughing ceased.

The duo approached my car like a pair of bulls just released from the pen. Blackwell rolled a toothpick around in his mouth and said, "You don't work here anymore, or did you forget?"

"Maybe she's lost," Foley added. "Are you lost, Miss Germaine?"

"If anyone's lost it's you, Foley," I said, "on the case you're working."

Foley opened his mouth to respond, but Blackwell cut in. "What are you doing here, Germaine? If you've come about the Holliday sisters, you're wasting your time. We don't share private information with *civilians*."

If his intention was to make me feel small, it would take a hell of a lot more to get there.

"I'm not here to ask for information," I said. "I'm here to give it. Though I'm starting to wonder if it was the wrong decision."

"Feel free to leave anytime," Blackwell said.

"I'll stay."

Blackwell tipped his head toward Foley. "Why don't you get going? I'll catch up with you later."

Foley looked disappointed. It was obvious he wanted to hear what I had to say. He gave Blackwell a two-finger salute and whistled as he made his way to his car.

Blackwell waited until Foley was out of earshot and then he turned toward me. "What's this private-eye business I've been hearing about?"

"I've decided to take on my own cases. Just because I no longer work for the department doesn't mean I can't still investigate."

"Your client is dead, which means your case is dead, just like Foley told you last night. Drop this little side gig of yours."

"I'm licensed, and what I'm doing is legal. I don't expect you to like it."

"Oh, I'll never like it. Stay away from my crime scenes. Got it?"

It was a promise I knew I'd never be able to keep so I steered the conversation in a new direction. "What do you know about Atticus Wolfe?"

"Who?" Blackwell asked.

Just as I assumed.

He knew nothing and had made no connection.

He tapped his foot on the pavement, thinking. "Wasn't she ahh ... like a serial killer way back when? She's doing time in Chowchilla, right?"

I nodded. "I went to see her today."

He raised a brow. "Why?"

"The crime scene for the Holliday sisters share some similarities to the crimes Wolfe committed in the '80s. Same staging of the body, same number written on a piece of paper. Pippa and Greer had a lock of their hair cut off just like Wolfe's victims did too."

I could tell he was trying extra hard to keep his cool and avoid unraveling. I imagined hearing something he should have known but didn't was a blow to his enormous ego. And even worse, the information had come from me, a woman he disliked. And I wasn't even done yet.

"I believe we're looking for a copycat killer," I said.

"Yeah, yeah. I got that. Doesn't mean you're right."

"Doesn't mean I'm wrong."

"And *we're* not a *we*. We're not working together on this case, or any other case. Not now or ever."

"I wouldn't suggest we team up even if you asked," I said.

"Good. I never will."

"I stopped by because I thought this information was something you should know."

"I'll say it again ... I don't need your help."

"Seems to me like you do, or you would have made the Atticus Wolfe connection already."

He grunted an agitated, "You done? I have more important things to do than to sit here listening to you."

So did I.

And yet I still found myself wanting to overshare.

"Wolfe confessed something to me today," I said.

"Oh yeah? And what's that?"

I paused, knowing how much easier it would be to keep it to myself. We weren't working together, but we were working toward the same goal—justice for Pippa and Greer. And to stop a killer before they struck again.

"Spit it out, Germaine," he said. "Or leave."

"I know what the significance of the number 1 means. Wolfe confessed to committing nine crimes, but there were only eight victims. Wolfe's first victim was her sister, Nancy. She died in a skiing accident, except now I know it wasn't an accident. I think the person we're looking for is—"

Blackwell raised his hand. "I've heard enough. Your attempt to throw us off the investigation so you can put on your cape and play the hero is cute. But that's all it is."

"I'm not trying to throw you off. There are no heroes here, just two women who didn't deserve to die. Everything I've told you is true."

"Go home, Germaine."

He turned around, shaking his head as he climbed into his truck.

He could see me as the town joke all he wanted. I'd done my duty. I'd tried to play a nice, clean game in the name of integrity. Now it was time to get dirty.

And I knew two amazing women who wouldn't laugh at me.

19

Y ou're hired," I said.

Lilia Hunter stared at me for a minute and then smiled. "You mean it? You want us to work together?"

"I do. You still interested?"

Hunter nodded. "Yeah."

I turned toward Simone. "What about you?"

Simone fist-pumped the air and said, "Hell yeah, I'm interested. Between the three of us, there's no case we can't solve."

"There's just one issue," I said. "Money isn't rolling in right now. It will take some time."

"I'm not doing it for the money," Simone said. "I have a day job. I'm doing this for fun, and for the look on Blackwell's face when he finds out three former detectives have teamed up together."

Not just detectives.

Three former *female* detectives.

"I am doing it for the money," Hunter said. "Well, not *just* for the money, but I meant what I said a couple of days ago about finding my own work. I'll bring in money doing all the boring stuff—background checks, infidelity investigations, surveillance."

"Doesn't sound boring to me," Simone said.

"I'd still like to help out with your cases too, Georgiana, starting with this one," Hunter said. "Where are you at with it?"

Not far.

Something I planned to change.

"Wolfe did an interview for *Serial Crime Magazine* a few months ago. I believe whoever killed the Holliday sisters read the article and decided to pick up where Wolfe left off. I'd like both of you to read the article tonight. I'll read it too, of course. In the meantime, I'll tell you everything I know so far."

Luka, who'd been resting his head on my lap, gave me a disgruntled look as I scooted away from him and stood up. I walked to the back of the Airstream and reached into my handbag, pulling out the notebooks I'd just bought and a couple of pens. I handed them to Hunter and Simone and then detailed everything I knew about the case so far.

"Wow," Simone said when I'd finished. "You've been busy."

"Your conversation with Wolfe was surreal," Hunter added. "She sounds … well, one part crazy, one part shrewd, and one hundred percent like someone I want to stay away from."

"She's one of the most cunning women I've ever met and far more dangerous than people realize. Her interview has turned someone into a killer. I think she wanted this to happen. And even though we don't have a lot to go on yet, talking to Wolfe has helped me form an idea about who we're looking for in my mind."

"Male? Female?" Simone asked. "What are we thinking?"

"I haven't ruled out either."

"You have an opinion though. I can tell."

"You're right. I'm leaning toward a woman. Men kill in more aggressive ways—shooting, beating, strangulation. Women are more prone to offing their victims with poison. Plus, I believe if it was a man, it's more probable he would have emulated a male serial killer, not a female."

"I agree," Hunter said.

Simone nodded.

"Our killer is similar to Wolfe in the way she stages the scene, clips the hair of her victims, saving them as mementos like Wolfe did, leaves a piece of paper with the number 1 written on it. What makes the two murderers different is the decision to kill two sisters. Wolfe killed her own sister, but no one except her brother knew that before now. And none of her other victims were related to each other."

"Could they have been connected in some other way?" Hunter asked.

"Good question. It's something we need to explore."

"I'll look into it," Hunter said.

"Good. I'd also like to know more about the family dynamic of Wolfe's victims. What was their homelife like? How many brothers and sisters? Were any of them adopted? Did they all get along? How did they meet Wolfe? How long did they know her before they were poisoned?"

"What can I do?" Simone asked.

"I need addresses. I need to know where Wolfe's other sister, Christine, is living, and I might also get in touch with Sarah Peterson, the woman who survived and is responsible for putting Wolfe in prison. She's not a priority though."

"Done," Simone said.

"I have a list of everyone who attended the party the night of Pippa's murder. I need someone to follow up with the guests, see if there's anything they remember that I should know about."

Simone looked at Hunter. "I'll take half, you take half. Deal?"

"Deal," Hunter said.

"As a side note, I found a pan of burnt brownies in Greer's oven, and the stove had been turned off. It's odd."

"If someone took the time to turn off the stove, why not take out the brownies while they were at it?" Simone asked.

"I thought the same thing. Because they were in a hurry?"

"If they were in a hurry, why turn the stove off at all?"

I aimed a finger at Simone. "Another good question, and one I've been asking myself. Here's my theory. The killer turned the stove off so the brownies wouldn't burn to oblivion and set the whole place on fire. Why? Because they wanted to make sure the police saw the staging of Greer's body."

"Killers and their stinking vanity," Simone said. "It's all about them, isn't it?"

"Not *all*. The killer may have also turned the stove off because of Cooper. It makes sense. Think about it. They've had two chances to harm the kid or to take him. Both times, they didn't. Why?"

"Good question," Hunter said. "You let us know when you figure it out."

"All day today I've been thinking about Wolfe leaving the number 1 on a slip of paper at each crime scene," I said. "It's ritualistic. Killing women and turning their head to face the number could have been euphoric, allowing Wolfe to relive Nancy's murder all over again."

"Damn," Hunter said. "She must have hated her."

"She did. And I want to know why."

20

I entered the house and found a note from Giovanni on the kitchen counter. Giovanni was out to dinner with his cousin Riccardo, who was staying in San Luis Obispo for a couple of days. The note said he'd be home before midnight. It also said he loved me.

And I loved him.

I thought back to what he'd said the night before about doing whatever was necessary for his family. It reminded me of the sacrifice Wolfe's brother had made for her. I wished he were alive so I could ask him why he'd done it, chosen his adopted sister over his own flesh and blood.

I ran a bath and then settled in bed with Luka by my side. Grabbing my laptop off the nightstand, I went to *Serial Crime Magazine's* website and bought a subscription so I could gain access to the article. At the top of the article's main page were three photos of Wolfe. One as a child, one on the day she was arrested, and a third showing what she looked like today. She may have changed a lot over the years, but one thing remained the same—her eyes. They were dead and hollow, devoid of emotion.

I leaned back and began reading.

Reagan: Tell me about your childhood.

Wolfe: There's not much to say about it.

Reagan: You were adopted.

Wolfe: Yes.

Reagan: What did you think of your adoptive parents?

Wolfe: They told me they adopted me to give me a good home, but that was a lie. Giving me a good home may have factored into the decision they made, but after they had three children, they tried to conceive a fourth for two years and couldn't. That's when they decided to adopt.

Reagan: Were you close to your siblings, Nancy, Daniel, and Christine?

Wolfe: Daniel.

Reagan: And your sisters?

Wolfe: We weren't close.

Reagan: Why not?

Wolfe: They didn't like the attention our parents gave me, and they didn't like me.

Reagan: Why didn't they like you?

Wolfe: Who knows? I never asked.

Reagan: Were they jealous of you?

Wolfe: I'd say so. Have you ever been trapped—locked inside a nook or cranny with no way out?

Reagan: I don't follow.

Wolfe: Of course you don't. Nancy and Christine used to play games with me and not the fun kind.

Reagan: Can you give me an example?

Wolfe: Once they asked me to sneak into the pantry and grab a bag of cookies while our mother wasn't home. As soon as I stepped inside and reached for the bag, they closed the door, locking me inside the pantry in the dark. I banged on the door, kicking and screaming for them to let me out.

Reagan: And did they let you out?

Wolfe: No. They stood in the kitchen, laughing.

Reagan: Are you saying they never let you out?

Wolfe: My mother did, hours later when she got home. My sisters told her they had no idea how I wound up locked inside.

Reagan: Did you tell your mother what happened?

Wolfe: I was never a snitch, not even as a child.

Reagan: How old were you at the time?

Wolfe: Old enough to have known better than to trust them.

Reagan: Why did they lock you up in the first place?

Wolfe: Isn't it obvious? They despised me.

Reagan: How did you feel when Nancy died?

Wolfe: I didn't feel a thing. She was dead. It made no difference to me.

Reagan: Your other sister, Christine, hasn't spoken to you or seen you since the day you were arrested. If you could see her now, what would you say?

Wolfe: Nothing. I'll never see her, and she'll never try to see me.

Reagan: Do you ever wonder how she's doing?

Wolfe: I don't wonder anything when it comes to her. I wish she was dead, just like Nancy. Do you want to know something, a little salacious tidbit to add to your article? I considered killing Christine once. Almost went through with it too.

Reagan: When?

Wolfe: A year or so after Nancy died.

Reagan: What stopped you?

Wolfe: Knowing she was suffering. Christine and Nancy weren't just sisters, you see. They were best friends. They did everything together. Christine had a mental breakdown after Nancy's funeral. Our parents sent her to therapy. It didn't work. She suffers every day of her life because Nancy is no longer in it. Seems like a far better punishment than death. Wouldn't you agree?

Reagan: You murdered eight women.

Wolfe: Nine.

Reagan: You claimed there were nine, and yet you've never identified the ninth victim. The police have reported there were no other similar murders at the time. Would you like to go on record and identify the ninth victim now?

Wolfe: That would be too easy, wouldn't it?

Reagan: Jill Jacobsen was your first victim. What made you decide to poison her?

Wolfe: She wasn't a victim.

Reagan: What was she, then?

Wolfe: Someone who deserved to die.

Reagan: Why?

Wolfe: You're asking the wrong question.

Reagan: What's the right one?

Wolfe: You're the one giving the interview. You tell me.

Reagan: Why did you take the time to get to know your victims before you poisoned them?

Wolfe: I wanted to see what kind of person they were, on the inside. I wanted to see if their life was worth living.

Reagan: You wanted to play God.

Wolfe: God has nothing to do with it.

Reagan: So you got to know each of the women you murdered … and then what? You killed them after they said something you didn't like?

Wolfe: Not all of them.

Reagan: Are you saying there were those you considered killing and then changed your mind?

Wolfe: Some people have redeeming qualities. Others don't. Some of the women I met back then are still alive. And the ones who aren't … well, they should have been better people.

Reagan: What criteria made you decide who was a good person and who wasn't?

Wolfe: Too many people in this world live to talk. They make everything about them and their own selfishness. Listen long enough, and people get comfortable. Listen even longer, and they reveal things, even though they know they shouldn't—all the imperfect, ugly sides of themselves, the sides they think you won't mind seeing, because they've gotten to know you. Or at least they think they have. They convince themselves that you've developed a bond with them, which makes you care more about who they are on the surface instead of the monster living inside of them.

Reagan: Can you recall the first time you ever thought about killing someone?

Wolfe: I was twelve. The teacher told us we were going to play a game. It was Valentine's Day, and she'd hidden a couple hundred plastic, heart-shaped containers on the playground. We went out, and I found eleven plastic hearts. They were filled with candy and change and that sort of thing. When we returned to class, I put mine into my backpack. When the dismissal bell rang, and it was time to go home, I opened my backpack to put my folder inside. All of my plastic hearts were gone except one. I looked around the room and noticed one of my classmates staring at me. One look at Sally's face, and I knew she'd taken them. I told the teacher. She laughed it off, said Sally would never do something like that. But she had. At recess the next day, Sally was swinging next to one of her friends. I walked up behind her and shoved her as hard as I could. I can still see her flying through the air and the terrified look on her face. She thought she was going to die. She broke a couple of bones, and all I could think about was how I should have pushed her even harder. I should have broken every bone in her body.

Reagan: Did you ever think about the people you killed, after you'd killed them?

Wolfe: They didn't deserve another thought. Why would I?

Reagan: Do you regret killing anyone?

Wolfe: I don't believe in having regrets.

Reagan: You cut a lock of hair from each of the women you killed and stored it in your freezer. Why?

Wolfe: Did you know all the hair on your head is dead? The hair inside the epidermis of the scalp is all that's still living. I liked having something I could preserve, even if it was dead, just like the women I'd murdered, who were also dead.

Reagan: A homicide archivist believes there are as many as two thousand active serial killers in the United States right now. I imagine there are others out there, others like you, who believe killing certain people is justified.

Wolfe: Are there other serial killers out there? Yes. Are they like me? No. What's your question?

Reagan: If you were released from prison tomorrow, would you kill again?

Wolfe: I could kill again without being released.

Reagan: I don't follow. Are you referring to your fellow inmates?

Wolfe: I have received a lot of letters over the years. Lots of people seeking my advice.

Reagan: What would you say to others out there, those like you, to dissuade them from acting on their impulses so they don't wind up in prison?

Wolfe: That's two questions, but I'll indulge you. You're implying all murderers get caught. They don't. It's not for me to decide the path a person chooses to take. But I will say this ... it should be taken for the right reasons. And above all else, no matter how smart a person thinks they are, there's always a risk of getting caught. Anyone considering going down the path I have must be ready to accept that.

21

I woke the next morning still thinking about the interview I'd read the night before. It was clear how someone reading it, someone full of angst, may have decided to act on impulses they otherwise would have suppressed. What I *didn't* know yet was whether we were dealing with a serial killer or if the murders would cease now that the Holliday sisters were dead.

The article offered new details into Wolfe's psyche.

Fact 1: She'd been fueled by rage from a young age.

Fact 2: She despised her sisters.

I changed out of my robe into a navy blouse and a black A-line skirt and went looking for Giovanni. I found him in the kitchen, wearing an apron, humming the tune of a Billie Holiday song, playing in the background. He pointed a spatula toward a chair at the bar and said, "Morning. I whipped you up some scrambled eggs, toast, bacon. Take a seat."

I stood on my tiptoes, gave him a kiss, and then sat down. He slid the plate of eggs in front of me.

"You're too good to me," I said. "How was your dinner last night?"

"It went as expected."

"Meaning?"

Giovanni fixed himself a plate of food and sat beside me. "Riccardo wants to do what he's always trying to do—expand the family business."

"What's his occupation now?"

"He oversees our construction companies."

"And how does he want to expand?"

"Wind farms."

It wasn't a bad idea. Wind farms had the potential to reach households in all fifty states over the next three decades, and even more worldwide.

"What do you think about the idea?" I asked.

"He needs to convince my sister first. She already said no. It's the reason why he came to me. He believes if I ask, she'll agree to it."

"Why did Daniela shoot the idea down?"

"Riccardo has trouble focusing on more than one thing at a time. I'll give our conversation some thought before I decide whether or not to get involved. How did everything go yesterday?"

I winked and said, "Oh, you know, just another average day. Interviewed a serial killer, argued with Blackwell, expanded my business."

"Sounds anything but average to me."

I stabbed a fork into my eggs and said, "This case is getting to me, you know? I feel so bad for Cooper. The poor kid must be going through hell right now."

"Have you seen him?"

"Not yet. I plan to stop by today. I talked to Tiffany Wheeler this morning. She's representing Alli Kane, Cooper's godmother. Blackwell and Foley are pushing hard to talk to the kid. I don't blame them. I was just hoping I'd get the chance to do it first."

"You better get moving, then."

I scooped up another forkful of eggs and nodded. I rinsed my plate in the sink, and a few minutes later, my cell phone rang. I glanced down at the caller ID. The number was unfamiliar. I pressed the answer button, said hello, and was greeted with an immediate, "You were right! That bastard lied to me!"

22

Who is this?" I asked.

"Laney St. James."

"Why are you calling?"

"I took your advice today."

"What advice?"

"We had a horrible fight last night. He was here, and he was getting all bent out of shape because I was pressing him about why he still hasn't told his wife their marriage is over. This was supposed to happen weeks ago. He should be living with *me* now—not her!"

She was screeching into the phone, talking so fast I couldn't keep up.

"Slow down, okay? You're saying you had a fight with the married man you've been seeing, right?"

"Yes, that's what I just said."

It *wasn't* what she'd just said.

"What happened after the fight?" I asked.

"He left, knowing how upset I was, which made me even angrier. I stewed about it all night. This morning I ransacked my entire place, trying to find what I'd done with the piece of paper you gave me. Took long enough, but I found the dang thing. I checked out the website you wrote down, and you're right. The A-hole never filed the paperwork. He's been lying to me all this time, telling me he loves me, needs me, would do *anything* for me, including leave his wife. I cannot believe it!"

I could.

What I couldn't believe was how naïve she was acting about it all.

I also wondered how much he'd benefitted on her dime.

She continued her rant. "You still want his name? I'll give it to you. It's Vincent Welles."

I jotted it down. "Thanks."

"Now you have it. What are you going to do?"

"What do you mean?"

"You're going to confront him, right?" she huffed out. "You just do me one favor when you do. You talk to his wife too. Make sure she knows all about me."

"Talking to Vincent isn't high on my priority list right now. The reason I asked for his name the other day was to verify your alibi. You said he was with you the night Pippa died. All I want him to do is corroborate your story. I'm not looking to get into the middle of your love triangle."

"You need to talk to him *and* her. Today. Understand?"

No, I didn't understand.

Push me any harder, and she'd soon regret it.

"I'll talk to him when I have time," I said. "If you're so adamant about her finding out about the two of you, why don't you tell her yourself?"

"Oh, no. You don't want me going over there. If I see him right now, he'll end up in the hospital, and I'll end up in jail."

I sighed.

How this woman managed to find a man willing to date her escaped me. She was a tornado hellbent on wrecking her way through everything in her path.

"Give me his number," I said.

She gave it to me and then started rattling off additional demands and telling me how she wanted the conversation to go.

I cut her off.

"I'll take it from here," I said. "And, Laney, unless I reach out to you for something else, don't contact me again."

23

Vincent Welles wasn't happy to get my call. He didn't confirm or deny his involvement with Laney. He didn't confirm or deny he was with her the night Pippa was murdered. He spent the entire call trying to end it, until I told him if he hung up on me, I'd stop by in person—something neither of us wanted.

Vincent simmered down, and I warned him about Monsoon Laney and suggested he steer clear of her. I didn't believe she'd stay away. She had no problem with confrontation, and it was obvious she had more than a few loose screws jarring around in her head. I suggested he come clean with his wife and then file a restraining order, even though I doubted it would save him. If Laney went on the warpath, nothing could.

As for whether they were together the night in question, he thought they were but wasn't positive on the date since a fair amount of time had passed. Either way, I'd ruled out Laney as a suspect for now. She was too reckless a person to coordinate organized murders, and I believed a fair amount of planning was involved. Laney also wasn't the poisoning type. If anything, she'd kill a person with her bare hands and take pride telling everyone about it.

I arrived in Paso Robles just after ten and was greeted at the door by a weary-looking Alli Kane. Last night's makeup was smeared all over her face, and she'd been crying. Her long, blond hair was tied back, but it didn't stop a handful of stray locks from sticking to the sides of her face.

We walked to the living room and sat down. Across from me was a wall-to-wall bookcase brimming with fiction books, most in the mystery, thriller, and science-fiction genres.

"You have a nice home," I said. "Do you live here alone?"

"My boyfriend lives with me. He's at work."

I pointed at the bookcase. "One of you likes to read."

"We both do. He's more into sci-fi. I'm the mystery buff. Ironic, right? I feel like I'm living a real-life mystery right now."

"How are you doing today?" I asked.

As soon as I'd said it, I felt like a first-rate idiot.

You can see how she's doing.

It's obvious.

"I haven't thrown up yet today, so I guess something's going right."

"How's Cooper?"

"He's started talking a bit, saying a few words here and there. I haven't asked him about what happened. Truth is, I don't know what to say. I've tried to get him to eat, but he just picks at his food. Guessing his stomach is all knotted up like mine."

"I'm sorry. I know how hard these things are."

"We'll get through it. My mom's flying in today to help. I can't always be here. I have to work. And my boyfriend's job is two weeks on, two weeks off. He's away right now."

"Where do the two of you work?"

"He's a ski instructor. When he works, he stays at the lodge. I run a PR firm."

"Have you heard from anyone at the police department today?"

"Yep. They called right before you got here. They asked me to bring Cooper in, but he freaks out every time I mention leaving the house."

"I'm sure they'd agree to come here instead."

She blew out a defeated sigh. "Is there any way I can stop them from talking to him? He's not up to it. Can't get him to change clothes, take a bath, or anything. He just stays under the covers in bed most of the time, hiding from this world and everything in it."

I'd had plenty of those same days myself.

"I wish we could give him more time, but unless the police solve the murder, they'll keep pushing to talk to him. As your lawyer, Tiffany can refuse the interview on his behalf, but the police will keep coming at you until you relent."

"I spoke to Tiffany this morning. She's working on stalling, giving Cooper more time to recover." She gritted her teeth and tossed her hands in the air. "Why don't they understand how freaked out he is right now and back off?"

She was irate and had every right to be.

"They understand," I said. "It's just … Cooper may have seen who murdered Greer, and if he could provide a description, it would make a big difference."

"Or he could have seen nothing. We don't know."

"You're right. We don't. When Greer called me right before she died, she told me someone rang her doorbell. When she went to see who was there, she found a note with the number 1 on it stuck to her door."

"Why would anyone do that?"

"To mess with her. I believe the killer wanted her to see the note before she died. My guess is the killer was hiding out nearby, watching. It tells me Greer had already been poisoned, and the killer waited until right before she died to ring the doorbell. There wasn't much time between her call and me arriving at her house. She was staged in a hurry. Cooper would have been there the entire time. He must have seen or heard something."

"Is this why you're here? You want to ask him about it?"

"If it's all right with you, I would like to see if he'll talk to me. My objective here is not to intimidate him or to make him feel pressured in any way. If you allow me a few minutes with him, I'll go easy. You can even sit with him while we're talking, or while I'm talking if he doesn't want to talk."

"If he doesn't want to talk, what's the point in putting him through it right now?"

"I learn a lot just by gauging a person's reaction to the things I say."

She nodded. "Can I think about it?"

As keen as I was to get any amount of time with him, she wasn't ready to give it to me yet. I decided to switch up the conversation up, removing him from the blaring spotlight of center stage.

"I heard you were supposed to raise Cooper. Not Greer. Why was he with her instead of you?"

"Once Greer realized what happened to Pippa, she packed all of Cooper's things and took him to her place. I called, tried going to see her in person. She wasn't rude to me or anything … she just said no. She wanted to raise him. She thought I would understand, and I did."

"Did she say you'd have to take her to court if you wanted custody?"

"I mean, yeah, she said something similar."

"Sounds rude to me. Did the two of you have a strained relationship?"

Alli grabbed a throw pillow from beside her on the couch, set it on her lap, and interlaced her fingers on top of it. "I've known Pippa and Greer since I was ten years old. We all hung out in school. We were close, but over the years, Pippa has been better at keeping in touch with me than Greer."

"Why did Pippa choose you to raise Cooper instead of her sister?"

"Greer never wanted kids. And she had no problem saying so."

"What about you?" I asked. "Do you have kids?"

She bit down on her lip and shook her head. "I went through a difficult divorce a few years back. During our five-year marriage, I had two miscarriages. The first one was bad, hard to get past. The second was impossible. Pippa knew how desperate I was to have a baby, and one day, she just blurted out that if anything happened to her, she wanted me to raise Cooper. I'm sure she thought the day would never come when she suggested it, and if it did, she knew I'd allow Cooper to be in Greer's life as much as she wanted him to be."

"Were you surprised when Greer told you she wanted to raise him?"

"At first. Then I started seeing it from her perspective. Pippa and Cooper were her whole world. Whether she planned to be a mother or not, he was family."

Now seemed like the right time to shift the conversation. "Do you know someone named Atticus Wolfe?"

"What kind of name is Atticus?"

"A rare one."

"I don't. Who is he?"

"*She* is a serial killer who is in prison."

"Why are you asking me about her?"

"The crime scenes were both staged to mimic Wolfe's murders back in the '80s."

"Wow. It's a crazy world we live in."

"When I went to see Trevor Armstrong, he told me he'd gotten back together with Pippa before she died. Did you know?"

"I did."

"Did Greer know?"

"I don't think so."

"Why didn't she like him?" I asked.

"I don't think Greer liked anyone who took time away from her sister. Didn't matter if it was a man or a woman. She could be possessive at times."

"What did you think of Trevor?"

"He was always nice to me. Pippa seemed happier with him than in any of her other relationships. I mean, yeah, I thought he was a bit old for her, but when they were together, they got along so well most of the time, you almost forgot the gap in their ages."

"What about Samantha, his daughter? Did you meet her?"

"I didn't. She was invited to come to dinner with us a couple of times, but she never showed up."

A phone sitting on the coffee table buzzed. Alli leaned down, stared at the screen for a minute, then rolled her eyes.

"It's the detective from the police department … *again*. This makes it the third call from him today." She sent the call to voicemail and leaned back. "You're right. They won't let up unless they talk to him."

I was about to reply when I heard what sounded like someone breathing behind me. I turned my attention toward the hallway and saw a sweet pair of eyes peeking at me from around the corner.

24

"Hey, pumpkin, are you hungry?" Alli asked.

Cooper nodded and then trotted off toward the kitchen. Alli followed. I stayed put. She hadn't given me the go-ahead to talk to him yet, and I wasn't about to mess up what might prove to be the perfect opportunity.

Alli rejoined me several minutes later. "I'm so glad he's eating, even if it is fruit snacks and sugary cereal. It's better than nothing."

"It is. He just needs time."

"My mother's pushing me to take him to a therapist, someone who specializes in kids who have been through trauma."

"My niece started seeing a therapist for something she went through a couple of years ago. It's making a difference. Seems like a great idea for Cooper."

"It might be. I'm just not sure he's up to it right now."

Her cell phone buzzed, and she reached for it but did not take the call.

"Are you kidding?" she shouted at the screen.

"Everything all right?"

"It's the police department—again!" She stood up halfway, craning her neck so she could glance into the kitchen and see how Cooper was doing. Then she turned back to me. "What if … since you're already here, *you* talk to Cooper, and then tell the cops what he said—*if* you can get him to talk."

I was certain Blackwell would still push to speak to Cooper himself, but it was the moment I'd been hoping for since I arrived.

My moment to speak with him.

"Sure," I said. "Let's give it a try."

I followed her to the kitchen and took a seat at the table, across from Cooper. Alli sat next to him. Cooper gave me a quick glance like he wondered what I was doing there, and then he went back to picking at the dry cereal on his plate.

Alli rubbed his back and said, "Cooper. You remember Georgiana, don't you?"

He stuck a few pieces of cereal in his mouth and behaved as if she hadn't said anything.

"Hi, Cooper," I said. "I remember eating Fruit Rings when I was a kid too. My favorite cereal was Cinnamon Life. Have you ever tried it?"

He shook his head.

I considered it a win.

Any response was better than no response.

"Has anyone ever taught you how to cook?" I asked.

He shook his head.

"When I was at your aunt's house, I found brownies in the oven. Someone had turned the stove off but left the brownies in the oven. Do you know anything about that?"

Cooper looked at Alli.

"It's okay," she said. "You can answer the question."

"It wasn't me," he said.

"Do you know who turned the oven off?" I asked.

He blinked at me, and his breathing became loud and heavy. "It was *her*."

"*Her?*"

"The girl in the mask."

Now we were getting somewhere.

Shocked, Alli pressed a hand against her mouth.

"What kind of mask?" I asked.

"A black one. It had holes in it."

"How do you know the person wearing the mask was a girl?" I asked.

"She whispered to me. She tried to change her voice to make it sound different."

"Different how?"

"I don't know … lower, like a man sounds."

"Do you remember what she was wearing?"

"Black stuff."

"Was she tall?"

"Yeah."

"How tall would you say … like Alli or me?"

"I dunno. Tall like a grownup."

"What did she say to you?" I asked.

"She put her hands on my shoulder. She told me to get inside the cupboard. She said someone else would come, and then I could get out."

"Did she tell you who else would be coming?"

He shook his head.

"Where was your aunt when you saw the girl?" I asked.

"On the ground in the kitchen. She fell down and she didn't get up."

A tear trailed down the side of his cheek. Alli reached over and wiped it off. "It's okay, honey. You don't have to keep talking if it's too much."

I wanted to elbow her in the side. This was the best information I'd received so far, and here she was, intervening. I took a mental step back and centered myself. She was just protecting him. I couldn't fault her for that.

Cooper looked at Alli and shrugged, as if indifferent, so I kept going.

"What happened after you got into the cupboard?" I asked.

"I don't know. She didn't talk anymore, and then she left."

"How do you know she left?"

"I heard the door shut."

Cooper glanced out the kitchen window and jumped off his chair, pointing and screaming, "She's out there! I saw her! She's here! She's coming to get me!"

I was on my feet, scanning the yard.

"Who's out there?" Alli asked.

"The bad lady!"

He started sobbing and took off down the hall. I reached for my gun and raced outside, looking for signs anyone was on or near the property. I found nothing. I walked back inside the house. Alli was waiting, leaning against the wall with her arms crossed in front of her. Not a good sign.

"He's locked the bedroom door," she said.

"I'm sorry."

"Yeah, well … did you see anyone out there?"

"No one."

"All this talk about what happened has him creating illusions in his mind. It's not good for him. He can't handle it. I think you better leave."

As she escorted me to the door, I glanced back, determined to get in one last question before I left. "Trevor told me Pippa called him one night after she'd had a bit to drink. She started talking to him about something in her past, something she regretted. Any idea what she was talking about?"

Alli shook her head. "Nope, I don't."

"Okay, well, if anything comes to mind, you let me know. In the meantime, be careful."

25

I sat in front of Alli's house, replaying the conversation with Cooper in my mind. It wasn't long before I was shedding tears of my own. The boy's mental state was fragile, and I worried I hadn't been as sensitive as I could have been. My goal was to find justice for his family, but he still had a long life to live. The road he needed to take to get past the trauma he'd experienced would be tough. It needed to be paved with love, compassion, and understanding from all those around him—including me.

The first thing I could do was to keep him safe.

I picked up the phone and called Simone.

"I was just thinking of you," she said. "How's the sleuthing going this morning?"

"It's going. What are you doing right now?"

"Just finished spin class."

"Are you working today?"

"I don't go back until Monday. Why?"

"I'm sitting outside Alli Kane's house. I just got finished talking with her and Cooper."

"The kid spoke to you? What did he say?"

I told her what had just happened, adding, "I think his imagination got the best of him, and he didn't see anyone in the back yard—not a person, anyway. Then again, there's a chance he saw something Alli and I didn't. That's what worries me."

"What can I do to help?"

"How do you feel about keeping an eye on the house while I meet with Foley and see if he's willing to send some officers out here?"

"Sure thing. Anything you need."

"Great. I'll hang around until you get here."

"Text me the address. I'll be on my way in fifteen."

"Thanks, Simone. And, ahh … one other thing. Let's keep this quiet. Meaning, unless Alli sees you hanging around, I'm not going to say anything to her yet."

"Not a problem."

"And if you do see anyone suspicious, use caution. Blackwell's already looking to shut me down—well, *us* down—now that we're in this together. The last thing I want is to give him an opportunity to do it."

26

Foley stepped into the office building, fixing his gaze on the surroundings.

"Thanks for meeting me here," I said.

I tried to make the sentiment sound genuine, even though I didn't care for the guy. He was the means to an end—an end who was about to be informed how much less he knew about the case he was investigating than I did.

"Why did you want to meet here?" he asked.

"Let's call it killing *no* birds with two stones," I said. "A little multitasking. I'm thinking of leasing this place, and I wanted to check it out first."

"Quitting the private-eye gig so soon? What a shame. What kind of business are you planning to open?"

"I'm not giving up the 'private-eye gig,' as you say. I'm expanding it."

The smug look on his face diminished. "How so?"

"I'm bringing on two more private investigators."

"Anyone I know?"

I nodded. "Simone Bonet and Lilia Hunter."

"Simone already has a job, and I thought Hunter didn't like detective work."

"Hunter didn't like working for Blackwell. It was her idea to work together. And Simone's doing forensic anthropology part-time now."

"Blackwell aware of this new development of yours?"

"If he is, he didn't find out from me."

"I'm not so sure I want to be the one to tell him."

"Why not? I thought the two of you were close."

Foley walked over to a dust-laden table, pulled a chair out, and sat down. He leaned forward, clasped his hands together. "*Close* is a word I doubt I'll ever use when it comes to Blackwell. He hasn't been the easiest person to be around this week, thanks to you."

I resisted the urge to crack a smile and pulled up a chair beside him. "Yeah, he's a tough one."

"On the phone you said you'd talked to the Holliday kid this morning. What did he say?"

"It wasn't a long conversation. He did shed light on a couple of things though. Greer's attacker talked to him. Well, whispered. She told him to get inside the cupboard."

"*She?* Huh. Anything else?"

"He was told someone else would come, and when they did, he could come out of the cupboard. By someone, I assume the killer may have meant me, that she was aware of the phone call Greer made to me just before her death."

"Was the boy able to describe the woman to you?"

"A little."

"What does she look like?"

"She was wearing a mask," I said.

"How's he so sure the perp is a woman and not a man, then?"

"He said she sounded like a woman."

Foley lowered his head and sighed. "Sounding like a woman doesn't make them one. Anyone can disguise their voice. Hell, you can download apps on your phone now that do all kinds of things."

"I'm just telling you what he told me."

"I will admit, after the way things ended between us the other night, I'm surprised you're telling me anything."

I leaned back, feeling a moment of truth coming. "I'll tell you the same thing I told Blackwell. We don't need to like each other to do what's right for this case—or any other case, for that matter. If sharing information with you helps get a case solved, I'll do it, even though I don't expect it to be reciprocated. I can be a bigger person, or I can *try* to be one, at least. The question is … can you?"

He paused a moment, sighed, and then rubbed his hands together like he was debating whether he should respond.

"I was talking to Officer Higgins this morning," he said. "I've been trying to get to know everyone at the department this week."

Why was he giving me this information?

"Okay," I said.

"I didn't know about what happened to your daughter … Fallon."

I wasn't sure why Higgins thought he needed to talk about it at all. But that's what people did—women and men alike. They talked. A little too much, in my opinion. "Is this why you seem more pleasant today? If it is, you don't have to be."

"No parent should ever have to suffer the loss of a child."

"I agree. I wouldn't want anyone else to experience what I've been through."

"So, it's true, then … what happened."

"If you're asking whether she slipped into the pool and drowned, yeah, she did. Can we talk about something else?"

He stared at me for a long time without speaking

"I feel like there's something you want to ask me," I said. "Go ahead, ask."

"All right. Why did you quit the department? Not the first time, after your daughter died, but the second time. I know Blackwell's version. I'd like to hear yours."

"It was a combination of things. If I tried to explain it, you'd be here for a while."

"I've got time. Give me the condensed version."

He was working extra hard to connect with me today. I wasn't sure if it was because he'd started to see me in a different way, or if it was all a pretense. There was no way of knowing yet, and therein lay my dilemma.

How much did I say?

How much did I not say?

He'd taken the time to meet with me today at a place of my choosing.

Why not give him a chance to redeem himself?

"I was a different person before my daughter died," I said. "Softer, more patient. I'm not suggesting I wasn't tough or brusque; I've always been those things. When Harvey talked me into coming back to the department a couple of years ago, I did it for my niece at first—to go after the guy who kidnapped her. And then, after I found him and she was safe, I suppose I stayed for me."

"Then you quit again. What changed?"

"The detective I was before my daughter's death wasn't the detective I was after. I was angry, grieving. That anger is still with me. I've tamed it to a degree, but I doubt it will ever be obliterated. It's always there, beneath the surface, looking for any opportunity to rise up."

"You quit because you were angry? Lots of people are angry, and they don't quit."

"I ran a man down a couple of years ago. Tapped him with the front of my Jeep as he was trying to escape. He wasn't hurt—not too bad. His name was Franko, and he'd murdered someone. He lit an office building on fire, not knowing anyone was inside. But someone *was* inside, and as the office worker screamed for help, Franko left him to die. I found Franko hiding out at his sister's house. He heard me coming and took off running down the street on foot. I could have chased after him, but instead, I got in my Jeep … and well, you know. I could have told myself he deserved it because he did …"

"Why do I feel a *but* coming?"

"When I took the job at the police department, I took an oath. I agreed to uphold certain rules, just like you did. When we break those rules and decide to handle a situation our own way, it disrespects everything we've been taught about law enforcement, and all the people we're there to serve."

He shrugged. "Sometimes rules need to be broken in order to get the job done."

He sounded like he'd stolen a page right out of Blackwell's playbook.

"I no longer work for the department, which means breaking a few rules every now and then is, ah, different now."

And because sometimes the worst people on this planet need to be kicked in the ass by the front of a Jeep.

"You didn't need to give up your career."

"I didn't give it up," I said. "I changed it. Police brutality has been in the news a lot more often over the last two years. And sure, I believe most officers and detectives mean well. They took the job to serve their city, their state, their country. To defend it. To preserve it. To make it proud. A few abuse their position though. Officers, detectives, police chiefs who are more interested in their own agenda than serving the best interests of the people. How well did you know Blackwell before taking this job?"

"Are you suggesting Blackwell is one of the *few*—a man who abuses the position he holds?"

"I'm suggesting you should get to know who you're working for, sooner than later. When Blackwell took over after Harvey retired, I spent a little time getting to know the new police chief. I refuse to work for a man whose morals I question."

"Speaking of morals you question, I assume Atticus Wolfe is on your list."

He'd dealt me a card I hadn't seen coming, and he'd done so on purpose.

"What about Wolfe?" I asked.

"Blackwell called the prison this morning, trying to get a one-on-one with her."

"And?"

"She refused. She has no interest in talking to him or to me."

I shrugged. "She seems to prefer women, both living *and* dead."

"Not women—*you*."

And there we were, arriving at what may have been the reason he'd indulged me all this time.

"What makes you think she prefers talking to me?" I asked.

"I don't think it. It's the truth. She told the prison warden to relay a message to Blackwell—a message for you."

"What message?"

"Blackwell asked me not to give it to you."

"Then why mention it at all?"

"I don't know."

"Yes, you do," I said.

"She wants to see you again."

"Is that the message?"

"Not all of it." He reached into his pocket, pulled out a slip of paper, and unfolded it. Clearing his throat, he read the note aloud. "'Women who hide from wolves never hide long. For the wolf is cunning. She sees all the shapes and shadows in the forest.'"

I sat for a moment, repeating the words under my breath.

"It doesn't make any sense, right?" Foley said. "The woman's insane."

"Don't be fooled. Everything Wolfe says has significance."

"All right, let's say I believe you. Explain your interpretation of her message."

"The woman, and I do believe it's a woman we're after … she isn't done killing yet. She's just getting started."

"How would you know that from the message?"

"Trust me, I just do."

27

Wolfe was trying to tell me the criminal I was chasing wasn't finished. I still wasn't clear on the motive behind the murders yet. When and where our murderess would strike next was anyone's guess. And the fact I still didn't know much about the woman I was hunting had spiked my anxiety.

After Foley and I went our separate ways, I checked in with Simone. Foley was sending an officer or two to keep an eye on Alli's house, something he and I both agreed should have happened the night Greer died. In the meantime, Simone had kept herself busy by searching the internet for information related to the case and by making some calls.

Simone told me Wolfe's sister Christine lived nearby in Harmony. I didn't know what purpose visiting her would serve other than helping me to profile the killer better. Which was, of course, a damn good purpose to have. I put it on my do-it-pronto list.

Simone had also spoken to a few of the guests at Pippa's cocktail party. Donovan Grant, one of Pippa's costars, told Simone about a housekeeper Pippa had fired before her death. The housekeeper, Adriana Simpson, lost her job after some cash went missing from Pippa's nightstand drawer. Pippa had shown up on set the following day distraught over the whole ordeal, and she told Grant all about it. It was a conversation he'd already had with Foley, which meant Foley would have already spoken with Adriana.

Now it was my turn.

Squeaky Clean Maids was located inside of a house that served a dual purpose—it was both a residence and a business. The business was on the main floor, and the living quarters on the second. I parked next to a van that had a custom vehicle wrap depicting a bath scene, complete with bubbles and a large rubber duck along with the name and contact information about the maid service.

I made my way inside and found a cheery woman with long, wavy, red hair whistling as she vacuumed the carpet. She was dressed in a pair of black skinny jeans and a red and white polka-dot, button-up blouse tied in a knot at the waist. She saw me and jumped forward, pressing a hand to her chest like I'd startled her.

She switched the vacuum off, placed a hand on her hip, and said, "Oh my goodness. Sorry. I didn't see you there. I hope you haven't been waiting long."

"It's no problem. I just walked in."

"What can I do for you?"

"I'm looking for Adriana Simpson."

She pointed at herself and smiled. "Then you're looking for me."

I offered my name and explained why I was there. She seemed unfazed and suggested we move to her office where we could both have a seat while we chatted.

"How long have you worked here?" I asked.

"I own the business with my sister. We opened a couple of years ago. Been doing well so far."

"Do you live here too? Upstairs, I mean? When I drove up, I noticed what I thought might be the living area through the window."

"We both live here."

It wasn't a big house. "No husbands or kids?"

"My sister's dating someone. It's getting serious. I think he'll pop the question sometime this year."

"And you?"

"I went through a rough breakup last year, and I'm still not anywhere near being ready to date." She went quiet for a minute. "Anyhoo, I, uhh, heard about what happened to Pippa and Greer. So sad. I can't believe it."

She'd called them by their first names, which indicated she may have had a personal relationship with them as well as a professional one.

"How long had you been employed by Pippa Holliday?" I asked.

"Not long. A couple of months. She'd just purchased the house when I started working for her."

"Did you also know Greer, her sister?"

"She stopped in sometimes at her sister's house when I was cleaning. I thought she was a nice woman at first, until she decided to have me fired."

The story Adriana was painting was different than the one Simone had told me.

"I heard Pippa accused you of stealing money," I said.

Her complexion changed from pink to red. "Yes, she did, but Greer is the reason I was fired."

"What did Greer have to do with it?"

"It's just … it's complicated."

"I have a healthy relationship with *complicated*. Try me."

She leaned back, folding her hands into her lap. "A couple of months ago, Greer was at the house, having me wash a few loads of her laundry because her washing machine was broken. Pippa arrived home earlier than usual, and I could tell she was stressed. Not her usual upbeat self."

"Did she say what was bothering her?"

Adriana leaned toward me and lowered her voice. "Yes."

We were the only people in the office, so I found the fact she'd whispered odd at first, until I thought about the residence on the second floor. Maybe we weren't alone in the building after all. Or maybe she was just a dramatic person. Hard to tell.

"Why was Pippa stressed?" I asked.

"Her boyfriend had planned on coming over for dinner."

"Are you referring to Trevor Armstrong?"

She nodded. "Greer wasn't supposed to be there. She hadn't called or let Pippa know she was coming over beforehand, so Pippa was shocked to find her hanging out at the house."

"You have a lot of information for a housekeeper who worked there for such a short time. How do you know all of this?"

"Pippa told me."

"I don't mean to be rude, but why would she tell *you*?"

"I mean, yeah, I was her employee. I get it. She was different than most of my clients though."

"In what way?" I asked.

"Most of the time, I'm just told what needs to be done or doesn't need to be done, or my client isn't at home while I'm there. Pippa was the chatty type, just like me. It didn't take long before we became friends. I *thought* we were friends anyway, until we weren't."

As far as stories go, she was doing a lot of skipping around, making it hard to follow what had changed between the day she first started working for Pippa and the day she was fired. "You started your story at the end. I need to hear the beginning."

She giggled and grabbed a handful of almonds out of a bowl on her desk. "Sorry, all I've had today is a piece of toast. I'm famished. And you're right. My stories *are* all over the place sometimes."

"It's all right."

I glanced at a large stack of tabloid newspapers on the ground next to her desk. It looked like there were a couple hundred in all. "You know a lot of what you read in these magazines isn't true, right?"

"I suppose not all of them are. Still fun going through them. These date back to the '70s. Bought them at a yard sale some months back. My sister and I laugh our heads off at some of the stories."

I had nothing more to add to the subject, so I changed it. "Tell me how you and Pippa became friends."

Before she could dive in, a heavyset woman opened a side door and entered the room, heading toward a copy machine in the corner. She smiled as she passed and said, "Hi."

"Hi," I said.

"Sorry to interrupt. Just trying to get the invoices sent out for the week."

Adriana turned toward the woman. "Margie, this is Georgiana Germaine, a private investigator. She's here to talk about the Holliday sisters."

"Oh, right. I'll get out of the way, then."

She pivoted and left the room.

Adriana shoveled another handful of nuts into her mouth and crossed her arms, resting them on the desk. "Okay, so ... I was about to leave Pippa's place one day. I went into the kitchen to tell her I was all finished, and as soon as I saw her, I could tell she'd been crying."

"Did she say why?"

"I asked if she wanted to talk about it, and she told me about Trevor."

"What about him?"

"Pippa said they had once dated, and they'd just started seeing each other again. It sounded like a good thing, so I couldn't figure out why she was so upset. Then she said she'd been keeping her relationship with Trevor a secret from her sister. Greer didn't like him."

I understood how Pippa's guilt over keeping a secret could have been weighing on her, but crying about it? Seemed to me something else was bubbling beneath the surface. Could it have had something to do with the comment she'd made to Trevor about a past regret?

"I know Greer wasn't fond of Trevor," I said. "But Pippa being distraught enough to get emotional over it … I don't know. It seems off to me."

"I thought the same thing when she told me. Maybe her emotions got the best of her because she felt guilty about lying to Greer that morning. Greer wanted to go to dinner together, and Pippa said she didn't feel well. It wasn't true. The truth was, Pippa already had plans with Trevor."

"I still don't have a clear picture of how Greer got you fired," I said.

"She didn't like me."

"How do you know?"

"Oh, come on. You're a woman. When it comes to other women, we always know. If another woman doesn't like you, you can sense it. She doesn't even need to say anything. It's a feeling, an instinct we get, deep down in our gut. You know the feeling I'm talking about, right?"

All too well.

It was like all women were hardwired with Spidey senses.

"Why didn't she like you?" I asked.

"Lots of reasons. She always kept tabs on Pippa, always wanted to know when she was coming or going."

"She was her assistant. It's an assistant's job to keep track of those things, isn't it?"

"Greer didn't just keep track of her. She bossed her around, told her what to do. And she was jealous."

"Of what, Pippa's success?"

"Jealous of the people in Pippa's life—Trevor, me, any of Pippa's other friends …"

"Why you?" I asked.

"A week before I was fired, Pippa invited Greer over for cocktails by the pool. It was my day off, and Greer didn't expect to find me there when she arrived, spending time with Pippa too. Greer asked what I was doing there. Pippa told her we were friends. Greer was irritated. You could see it on her face. And then, right in front of me, she told Pippa it was a bad idea to be friends with people who worked for her. What a stupid thing to say, given the fact Greer worked for her too."

"How did Pippa respond?"

"She ignored the comment and offered her sister a drink, tried to lighten the mood."

"Did it work?"

"I thought so, until the following week when Greer brought over her laundry."

"The same night Pippa had plans with Trevor."

"Right. Greer saw Pippa and me whispering in the kitchen about why Greer was there. The next thing I know, Greer was pulling Pippa aside telling her she had a thousand dollars in her purse when she arrived at the house, and now it was gone. She accused me of taking it. Pippa laughed it off, saying she thought Greer had misplaced it. A few days later, Greer called me up and told me I was fired. She said if I showed up at the house again, she'd call the police."

"Did you ever speak to Pippa about it?"

Adriana shook her head. "I was upset, so I didn't. I should have."

"You're right. You should have. For all you know, Pippa never fired you in the first place. Greer did. And who knows what Pippa thought, what Greer had told her. Pippa could have thought you just up and left, and she didn't want to deal with it anymore."

"Once I calmed down enough, I wanted to give Pippa a call. I put it off a few times, and then I found out she was dead."

"Where were you the night she was murdered?"

She narrowed her eyes but seemed prepared for the question. "I was here, with my sister. You can ask her. You wouldn't be the first one. A detective came by the other day. He talked to me, and he talked to Margie."

"Do you have any idea who wanted Pippa dead?"

It was a standard question, one I always asked. It rarely led anywhere. Imagine my surprise when she said, "Yeah, I can think of one person. I was pulling in to clean one afternoon, and Pippa was sitting in the car in front of her house. There was another woman with her, and it was obvious the woman was upset. Pippa made eye contact with me and waved me off, like she didn't want me to get involved. So I didn't. And now, when I think back on it, I wonder if the woman I saw had anything to do with Pippa's murder. Maybe if I'd stepped in, Pippa would still be alive today."

"Even if this mystery woman was responsible, what happened isn't your fault."

"Maybe one day I'll believe it. Maybe if I hadn't stopped talking to Pippa, I would have known what was going on in her life and somehow been able to stop it."

"Tell me about the woman you saw. How old? What did she look like?"

"I never saw her face. I pulled into the driveway and parked next to Pippa's car. The woman was facing away from me, talking to Pippa. She had blond hair ... or maybe reddish-blond hair. Long, straight. She was slender. Not too slender, but maybe fifteen pounds less than I am."

"If you didn't see her face, how do you know she was upset?"

"She kept throwing her hands in the air and jabbing her finger at Pippa, and she was yelling … about what, I'm not sure."

"When did this happen?"

"A little over a month ago, I'd say."

One month.

Not long after Wolfe's article was published.

28

As the sun faded into the horizon and the gentle breeze of evening kicked in, I received a call from Harvey. My mother was at a movie with a friend, making it the perfect time for us to catch up about the case. I arrived at the house and found him kicked back in his recliner, tuning in to an episode of one of his favorite shows—*Jeopardy*.

Harvey smiled when I entered the room and waved me over. "Come on in and have a seat. Want a cup of tea, or how about something stronger? Not sure what we have kicking around this place, but I'm sure I could rustle up a bottle of wine if I poked around the kitchen."

"Earl Grey tea would be great."

"You got it. Be back in a jiffy."

He shuffled past me and walked into the kitchen, returning a few minutes later with a mug of Earl Grey topped with a dash of milk, just the way I liked it. He resumed his position on the recliner, wiggling a glass in my direction and smirking. "Found a bottle of whisky in the cabinet above the fridge and decided what the hell, your mother's not here. Best live a little while she's away."

I laughed.

He set the glass down and smacked his hands together, rubbing them like he was warming them over a fire. "All right. Let's get to it. How's the old broad doing these days?"

I filled him in on my visit with Atticus Wolfe.

"You were right," I said. "Wolfe is smart. She's thrilled someone's out there, picking up where she left off."

Harvey clicked the remote control, turning the television off. "Funny how quiet she's stayed all these years, refusing interviews, in-person visits. Her brother's death has her rethinking a few things, I reckon."

Things like what she wanted her legacy to be after she was gone.

"I agree. From what I gather, Wolfe doesn't want to fade away, letting the history of who she is, or who she *was*, die right along with her."

Harvey swallowed a mouthful of whisky and nodded. "Think you'll see her again?"

"I don't know. Maybe. I forgot to mention something she said. She told me my dad had visited right before he died. He thought he'd figured out why the number 1 was so significant to her. I assume what he realized was what she confessed to me—her sister's skiing accident was no accident. Did he ever say anything to you?"

"Sure did."

"Why didn't the department pursue it?" I asked.

"Truth is, Wolfe was already in prison for life, and your father couldn't prove the sister, Nancy, had been murdered. Even I wasn't sure about his suspicions. He spent weeks trying to prove them, but in the end, it was nothing more than a hunch. He didn't take it to the chief of police because the department was satisfied with Wolfe's conviction. They weren't interested in dredging up the past. She was doing time for the murders we investigated. They wanted to move on."

I sipped on my tea, thinking about what he'd just said. "Makes sense. Hey, did you and my dad ever talk to Christine, Wolfe's other sister?"

"We tried on several occasions. She had no interest in speaking to us."

"I have her address, and I've been wondering if she'd be willing to talk to me."

"All I can say is ... good luck. From what I recall, she's not a pleasant woman."

"*Not pleasant* seems to run in the family. With the sisters, at least."

"Sure does. What's happening with your investigation? Got your eye on any suspects yet?"

"Speaking of hunches, all I have to go on right now are my own. I believe we're looking for a woman, and so far, I have a few on my radar, starting with Samantha Armstrong. She's Pippa's boyfriend's daughter. She wasn't thrilled her father was in a relationship with someone who wasn't age-appropriate for him."

"I suppose most women in her position would feel the same way."

"Pippa invited Samantha to visit her on the set one day, and she met Greer. When Greer found out who she was, she changed her attitude toward her. She went from being polite and chatty to straight-up rude, according to Samantha."

"Why?"

"Greer didn't like Samantha's father. She thought he was paranoid and possessive of Pippa. I've met him, and he doesn't seem that way to me—unless he's great at hiding it. Before Pippa's death, they rekindled their relationship, something Pippa kept from Greer because she didn't think she'd approve."

"Huh. Who else are you looking at?"

"On a lesser scale, Alli Kane. She's known Pippa and Greer since childhood. According to Pippa's will, Alli was supposed to be given parental rights for Cooper, Pippa's son, in the event of her death. Instead, Greer took him and told Alli she'd have to fight her in court to get custody."

"What you're saying is … Greer was a real piece of work."

The more I learned about her, the more I believed it.

"I've also been wondering if Alli was the kind of friend to Pippa she claims to be. Oh, and there's another thing. I can't stop thinking about a comment Trevor made when I met with him. He said Pippa made an aloof statement about a big regret she had from her past. I asked Alli about it, and she acted like she had no clue what I was talking about. I'm not sure I believe her."

"Two solid suspects. You have your work cut out for you with this one."

"I'm not even done yet. Then we have Adriana Simpson, Pippa's housekeeper. I talked to her today. She was fired just weeks before Pippa's murder. She claims she and Pippa had become friends and Greer didn't like it."

"I can say one thing … all your suspects have one thing in common."

I nodded. "They all disliked Greer. And yet, Pippa was murdered first."

Harvey leaned back, tugging at his chin.

"What?" I asked. "What are you thinking?"

"You reminded me so much of your father just now. By your tone of voice, I assume you have your own theory."

He was right.

I did.

"Wolfe killed Nancy and left her other sister, Christine, alive so she could spend her life suffering over the loss of Nancy. It was Wolfe's way of dealing with their mistreatment of her. Her sisters left her out, made fun of her, teased her, made her feel like an outsider instead of part of the family. What if our killer is doing the same thing?"

"Wouldn't she have left Greer alive, then?"

"Her plan could have been to leave her alive at first. Maybe she lacked the impulse control Wolfe had. With this new killer, Wolfe 2.0, killing Pippa may not have been enough. She may have needed Greer to die too. What's more, Wolfe didn't stop with her sister. She killed several other women—women she didn't know well. Wolfe is the perfect example of a true serial killer. Wolfe 2.0 might not be."

"And you think the woman you're seeking differs how?"

"Wolfe was a mission-style killer. She believed her murders were justified, that she was killing women who deserved to die. Wolfe 2.0 *might* be motivated in the same way, but what if she isn't?"

"What are you suggesting?"

"I'm thinking payback for something she endured, a crime of passion or revenge."

Harvey tapped his thumb on the wooden armchair. "Did Greer and Pippa have any other siblings?"

"They didn't. It was just the two of them."

"Parents still alive?"

"They are. They do volunteer work in Africa. They came for the funeral and turned right around and flew back out again."

"No one else to murder in that family, then. Sounds like the parents weren't close to their children."

"I don't think they were. All this week I've been focusing on Pippa, her life, those around her, who liked her, who didn't. From what I've learned, Pippa was sensitive and kind, someone who tried to do right by others. She became friends with others based on who they were on the inside, not their social status—rich, poor, it didn't matter."

"And Greer differs how?"

"Everyone I've talked to has had similar things to say about her. She was jealous, bossy, and didn't like it when things didn't go her way. She was the ringleader, the dominant one."

"What does that tell you?"

"I need to focus on Greer's past just as much as Pippa's, if not more."

"You're on the right track. It's what I would do if I were still a detective."

"Going back to our conversation about Wolfe, she gave Blackwell a message to give to me today. She said women who hide from wolves never hide long. For the wolf is cunning, and she sees everyone in the forest."

Harvey mumbled some of the words out loud. "Women never hide for long … she sees everyone. Everyone … everyone involved."

"I take it to mean Wolfe 2.0 will kill again until *everyone* on her hit list is dead," I said.

"Could be."

"I need to figure out the motive of these crimes. The motive will lead me to the killer. I know it."

He reached out, patting my arm. "You'll get there. Trust your gut just like you always have, and before you realize it you'll—"

Before he could finish, we heard what sounded like something being smashed outside, in front of the house. We leapt up, barreling toward the front door. I got to it first and headed out, aiming my gun in the direction of the sound we'd heard. Harvey wasn't far behind with his rifle. I searched the area, seeing no one. Under the streetlamp, I got a good look at my car. The driver's-side window was shattered, and three small pieces of paper were stuck to the windshield along with a message typed in red.

HELLO
DETECTIVE
GERMAINE

29

I leave for three hours, and *this* is what I come home to, Harvey? I cannot believe it." My mother tapped a foot on the pavement and then jerked her head in my direction—a move that had a slight *Exorcist* vibe. "And *you*, Georgiana ... what is the meaning of this ridiculous message and vandalism to the car your grandmother left you?"

The car, a '37 Jaguar SS 100, seemed to matter a little more to her at present than how I was doing, even though I knew it wasn't true.

"Mom, I—"

"What have you gotten yourself into? *This* ... this right here is why I can't sleep at night. I stay up into the wee hours sometimes worrying about this detective business. You keep telling me you're not in danger, and yet, here we are."

"Now, Darlene," Harvey began, "it's not her fault someone—"

"*You*," Darlene said, aiming a finger at Harvey's face, "should care more about the situations she's gotten herself into in recent years. Think about how I'd feel if I lost her. Would you? Let someone else's child play cops and robbers. Not mine."

"All I'm saying is, you don't need to be so hard on her, all right? What she chooses to do for a living is her choice. She's a grown woman, for heaven's sake."

Harvey was just trying to help, but he wasn't helping at all.

Each comment seemed to infuriate her a little bit more.

Foley, who'd arrived minutes before, was standing off to the side, observing the damage to my car. He piped up with, "I must say, this is some secret admirer you've got yourself, Germaine."

Knowing he'd witnessed my mother's verbal tongue-lashing couldn't have been more embarrassing.

"I'm sure you're getting a good laugh out of this," I said.

"I wasn't laughing."

"You want to though. I can tell."

My mother pivoted and stormed toward the house, mumbling a slew of words under her breath that no one could understand. As soon as the front door slammed shut, Foley burst out laughing.

"Go ahead," I said. "Get it all out. I'm sure it makes you feel better."

"Oh, it does."

"Look, I called you because I figured you may want to have Silas dust the car for prints."

"I'm still trying to decide what I want to do here."

"What do you mean? The killer is trying to send me a message. Why wouldn't you process this the same way you would any other crime scene?"

"We don't know who's responsible. Could be the person I'm investigating, or it could be someone else."

"It *isn't* anyone else."

"How can you be so sure? Did you see who did this? Are there any eyewitnesses? Any neighbors see what happened?"

"I haven't had time to ask. *You* were my first call. Maybe you should have been my second, or maybe I shouldn't have called you at all."

He waved a hand in front of him. "Now hang on a second. I'm not saying you're wrong."

"Then what are you saying?"

"Is it possible you have other enemies? In the short time I've known you, I've noticed you speak your mind. Not sometimes. All the time. I'm sure you've offended your share of people over the years."

So much for the bonding session we'd had earlier. While he wasn't being a complete jerk, he had partial jerk down pat.

Harvey stepped up beside me. "She called *you*. She didn't have to do it. If you want to know about her character, that's all you need to know."

Foley went silent for a moment and then extended a hand toward Harvey. "Nice to meet you. Everyone speaks highly about you at the department. I've never met a group of people who respected their boss as much as they respect you."

"Well, thank you," Harvey said. "They're a great bunch."

Foley turned toward me. "I do appreciate the call, Germaine. I'll get Silas on the phone and get him out here."

I nodded and said, "If you'll excuse me, I have some neighbors to question."

30

Despite my independent ways, I was starting to think it wouldn't be such a bad idea to accept Giovanni's suggestion of having Peppe around from time to time. The killer was keeping tabs on me. The fact she'd chosen to make contact at my mother's house was a calculated move. A move that said: *I know all about you.*

I dropped my car into the auto repair shop the following morning and borrowed Giovanni's Rolls-Royce Wraith, the perfect ride for the long day ahead. My first stop was at Wolfe's sister's place, a two-story, boxy beach house painted a bright shade of coral. I exited the car and paused, taking a moment to admire her breathtaking, unobstructed view of the ocean. It wasn't long before a woman inside the house moved the curtains to the side and eyeballed me. Then the deadbolt on the front door clicked.

Dressed in an oversized striped sweater and loose-fitting jeans, the woman walked outside, using a cane to help her get from point A to point B. She made it to the edge of the porch, moved a hand to her hip, and said, "What are you doing? And why are you parked in front of my house?"

"I was admiring your view. It's amazing."

"Yeah, well … if you head to the end of the street there's an empty lot. You can stare all you want, and then you won't be trespassing."

"I'm not here to see the ocean. I'm here to see Christine. Is that you?"

She used her cane to point at a placard attached to the front of her mailbox: NO SOLICITING.

"I'm not a solicitor."

"Then who are you?"

"A private investigator. I'm looking into the murders of Pippa and Greer Holliday."

"Ahh, I see. Awful, what happened to those women. Shame about the young boy too. No telling what kind of life is in store for him now. Not a good one, I'd say. What are you doing here? What do you want?"

There was no easy way to say what I needed to say next, or to gauge what her reaction would be once I did. Based on our interaction so far, I wasn't sure how long I'd last before she booted me off her property.

"Not all the details from the murders have been released to the press yet," I said. "Details like the victims' bodies being staged the same way your sister staged her victims decades ago."

Christine grunted, "Sister? She's no sister of mine. Never was, for that matter."

"Why? Because she was adopted?"

"Because she's a no-good psycho. Always was; always will be."

"Are you aware that she gave an interview not long ago? It's the first time she's agreed to talk to anyone other than your brother since she's been in prison."

"What she does, or how she's doing, or who she's talking to or not talking to ... none of it matters to me. If you came here hoping for a cup of coffee and a casual conversation about the old days, you're wasting your time *and* mine."

She turned and headed back toward the house without another word.

I followed. "Look, I'm trying to find out who killed the Holliday sisters and why. And since the person who committed these crimes is imitating your sister's crime scenes, I'm convinced learning more about your sister will point me in the right direction. I'm getting close to finding the killer. I know I am. Any help you can give me would—"

"If you want answers, you should talk to her, not me."

"I already have."

She raised a brow. "What do you want with me, then?"

"Have you ever heard your sister being described as a mission-oriented killer?"

"Nope. Can't say I have."

"She believed killing those women was necessary. She's convinced herself the world is a better place without them in it. In her eyes, she was doing everyone a favor by ending their lives."

Christine twirled a finger in the air. "Whoop-dee-doo."

"I'd like to know how she became the person she is today. What was her trigger, her motivation to kill?"

"She didn't *become* anything. She was born evil. Look at her. Look at what she's done."

What about you and what you've done?

"Was she locked inside of a pantry as a child by you and your sister?" I asked.

"A time or two. It was so long ago. Hard to remember."

"I heard you and Nancy locked her in that pantry for hours, leaving her there, begging to be let out. You could have unlocked the door, but you didn't. You allowed her to suffer, to wait until your mother returned home. Why?"

She swished a hand through the air. "Whatever we did when we were kids was all just a bit of fun."

"Would it have been fun if the same had been done to you? I'm not sure Atticus sees it that way."

"Who cares how she sees it?"

"Why refuse to let her out of the pantry?"

"I guess we thought it was funny."

"Funny? Were you jealous of her?"

Christine blew out a full-bellied laugh. "Jealous? Of what?"

"I'm guessing she wasn't treated the same way by your parents as the rest of you were. Am I wrong?"

Christine set her cane to the side, leaned against the front door, and crossed her arms, staring out at the ocean with an expression that made it seem like she was reliving the past in her mind—a past she'd rather forget. "When Addy was a child, she was scrawny and pale. It seemed like she was always getting sick, being taken to the doctor for one thing or another. Because of it, my mother doted on her, treated her like she was a fragile little doll. Sometimes Nancy and I felt invisible, even though *we* were blood. *We* were family. Not her. Did we tease her here and there because of it? I suppose we did. But we never hurt her."

Hurt. Pain. Suffering.

Christine's declaration of "we never hurt her" was in relation to physical pain, and I wasn't so sure that was true. But what about mental pain? I imagined a child who had idolized her older sisters at first, until they started abusing her. Locking her in the pantry. A little shove here, a little shove there.

A shove that said:

We don't like you.

You're unwanted.

You'll never be one of us.

And then the once scrawny, gaunt child grew up, grew bigger, grew angry, and the day came when she decided to make them pay.

And pay they had, in more ways than Christine seemed to realize.

I wondered if Pippa and Greer were murdered for something they had done. Yes, they must have been, and it was the cause of Pippa's deep-rooted regret.

"There's something you should know about the day Nancy died," I said.

"What about it?"

"It was no boating accident."

She blinked at me, like she expected me to say I was joking, that I hadn't meant what I'd just said. When I didn't flinch, she said, "What are you talking about? It *was* an accident. Daniel said so, and he wouldn't lie."

"Not even if it was to cover for something Atticus had done?"

"Atticus wasn't on the boat at the time. She was shopping. I remember the new dress she was strutting around in when she got home, before either of us knew what had happened at the lake."

"Whatever story you were told, Atticus is telling a different one now, and I believe her. When she was arrested and charged for eight murders and one attempted murder, she stated she'd killed nine women altogether."

"Doesn't mean it was Nancy. Could have been anyone."

"At each one of her crime scenes, she left a slip of paper behind with the number 1 written on it."

"Yeah, so?"

"The number 1 refers to her *first* victim. It wasn't Jill Jacobsen. It was Nancy."

"No. I'm not going to stand here and listen to this nonsense any longer. Addy didn't like us any more than we liked her, but to kill Nancy over a few hard feelings when all we ever did was ..."

Christine went silent, cupping a hand over her mouth, her legs shaking as she lowered herself onto a chair. I hopped onto the porch and took hold of her arm as she struggled to take a seat. "Here, let me help you. Are you all right?"

She leaned back and closed her eyes, saying nothing for a time. Then she looked me in the eye. "It's been so long ago now, I'd almost forgotten."

"Forgotten about what?"

"Nancy and Addy got into a nasty fight that morning, right before Nancy and Daniel went to the lake. Nancy had showered for so long, by the time Addy got in, there was no hot water left. Addy was standing in the shower, trying to wash the shampoo out of her hair when it went cold. She started shouting at Nancy, and Nancy snuck into the bathroom and snipped off a chunk of Addy's hair."

She. Cut. Her. Hair.

Everything about Wolfe's crime scenes had been significant, each item a window into her own past.

"When Daniel talked about what happened on the boat, did anyone ever question his story?" I asked.

She shook her head. "He was the most kind, genuine person I've ever known. No one would suspect he'd lie about it."

"Years later, when Addy was arrested, the news would have reported the locks of hair she'd taken as souvenirs over the years. You never made the connection between the murders and what happened the day Nancy died?"

"Of course not. We were humiliated. I tried to stay as far away from it as possible." Christine grabbed her cane and pushed herself back to a standing position. "I've said all I want to say. If what Addy said about Nancy is true, I'm just glad my parents didn't live long enough to hear about it. If you see her again, give her a message from me, would you?"

"What message?"

"Tell her every night I pray to wake up the next morning and find out she's died in some awful, horrible way."

"Oh...kay."

"She killed my sister. She deserves to be dead."

31

Over the next couple of hours, I took a long scenic drive along the central coast to Monterey. The picturesque city was a one-time hub for the sardine-packing industry. Now the streets brimmed with restaurants and gift shops and cheery locals who beamed with pride about the late, great John Steinbeck, whose childhood home was a short drive away.

Donna Reagan, the woman who interviewed Wolfe for *Serial Crime Magazine* lived in Monterey, on a houseboat with the name *Static Flow* painted in gold cursive on the side. Beside the name was a mermaid holding a trident with bolts of lightning shooting from the tips.

I approached the boat and found Donna sitting on a chair on the top deck, her laptop open, typing away as the floppy, oversized hat on her head wafted in the gentle breeze. She turned when she heard me coming and stood, sliding the laptop into a beach tote, and then slinging the bag over her shoulder.

She acknowledged me with a quick wave and smiled, and then made her way down to the main deck.

"You're the private investigator who called, right?" she asked.

"I am."

"Are you hungry? I was just about to pop below for a snack."

"I stopped and got something on the way here, but you go ahead."

She nodded, and I followed her to the lower cabin. While she whipped up a plate of cheese and crackers, I hopped onto a barstool.

"Your boat is nice," I said.

"Thanks."

"What made you decide to live this way?"

"I'm happiest when I'm close to the ocean, and since I can't afford a house with an ocean view, not yet anyway, I figure this is the next best thing."

I pointed to a shelf lined with a handful of miniature clocks. "Nice collection."

"Thanks. I pick them up here and there on my travels."

She wrapped up the remainder of the cheese, tossed it into a shelf in the fridge, and then joined me, removing her hat to reveal a brown pixie cut.

Combing her fingers through her hair, she said, "These last several weeks have been hard. I've been feeling guilty, you know?"

"About what?"

"I've traveled the world over the last several years doing all kinds of interviews, and I never thought anything of it. I didn't stop to consider someone might read my article and it would prompt them to go out and start killing people."

"If your interview made someone act on their impulses, it has nothing to do with you."

"It shouldn't, but still … what if I hadn't interviewed her? Maybe this wouldn't be happening right now."

"Serial killers are interviewed all the time in the paper, in magazines, on podcasts, on TV. There are countless television shows and movies in the crime genre. If someone wanted ideas, there are plenty of other places to look."

She grabbed a cracker, spread a generous amount of brie over the top, and said, "I guess you're right. Nothing like this has ever happened to me before. Hard not to feel somewhat responsible."

"Well, you're not."

"I still can't believe she agreed to be interviewed. I knew it was a longshot when I asked. I never expected her to say yes."

"How much of the conversation was published in the magazine?"

"Most of it."

"What was left out?"

She stuck a couple olives in her mouth and said, "Anything Atticus Wolfe didn't want printed, I didn't print."

"Why not print everything?"

"Prior to accepting the interview, she had an agreement drawn up that said anything she didn't want in the article would get cut out. After the interview, she went over my notes on everything we'd discussed and told me what to exclude."

"What did she ask you to leave out?"

"I tried to talk to her about a letter she'd received from Sarah Peterson, the woman who survived the attack, and she shut me down."

"How did you hear about the letter?"

"About a week before the interview, I visited Sarah. She's in a senior-living retirement community now, living a quiet life. I was hoping she'd tell me about her experience through her own eyes—what she saw, what she went through, how she felt back then, how she feels now."

"What did Sarah say?"

"She didn't want to talk about it. Any of it. She said she'd let it go and moved on a long time ago. She didn't think it was healthy to dig it all up again. According to her, the letter was the last thing she needed to do before she had closure. When I brought it up to Wolfe during our interview, she asked if I'd been to see Sarah. The notion I may have seen Sarah bugged her. I could tell. So, I lied and said it was a rumor I'd heard."

"And how did that go over?"

"It didn't. She saw right though my BS and almost ended the interview on the spot."

"How did you convince her to keep going?"

"I apologized, told her I didn't want to upset her, and then I talked about the one thing I knew mattered to her most, given the research I'd done on her—Daniel."

Nice save.

"Did Sarah tell you what the letter said?" I asked.

"It was short, no more than a few sentences. She wanted to say her peace and be done with it. She told Wolfe she forgave her for what she did, that she's a different person now than she was back then."

"Different how?"

"I don't know. Better, I guess?"

"Wolfe murdered women she believed deserved to die, but no one knows what criteria she based that on or why she let some women live and not others."

She hopped off the barstool, walked to the kitchen sink, and rinsed her plate. "I looked into Sarah's background. During the time she knew Wolfe, she had a drug problem. She was addicted to meth. She'd been arrested a few times. During one of her stints in jail, she found out she was pregnant. She carried the baby to term, but he was stillborn."

"I'm guessing Wolfe knew about what happened with the baby."

"She did. Sarah confided in her not only about the baby being stillborn, but about the fact Sarah continued her meth habit during the pregnancy."

That's why Wolfe wanted to kill her. If I took a closer look at her other victims, I was sure I'd find they all had similar stories.

"I know why the copycat killer is staging the murders to resemble Wolfe's crime scenes," I said.

Donna faced me, intrigued. "Do tell."

"She admires Wolfe and her reasons for killing the people she did. By staging the scene in a similar way, she's paying respect to Wolfe. Whoever she is, I bet she had a personal relationship with Pippa and Greer. They weren't random strangers. They were people she knew. She may not have known them well, but she knew them."

"What makes you think you're looking for a woman?"

"Everything about this case. Half of all female killers prefer poison and smothering over guns and knives. They tend to kill over long periods of time. Females also tend to kill people they know."

Donna leaned against the kitchen counter, taking in all I'd said. "Huh. Okay then, I have a question for you."

"Shoot."

"Why do you think Wolfe wouldn't allow me to talk about Sarah's letter in my article?"

It was an easy question, with an even easier answer.

"Because Wolfe wants to see Sarah the same way she always has—as someone who deserves to die. Everyone sees Sarah as a victim because of her near-death experience. They feel sorry for her and what she went through. Imagine how they'd feel now to learn the woman they sympathize with forgave her attacker years later. May as well put her on a pedestal alongside Mother Teresa."

Donna laughed. "Ahh, yes. Makes sense. Wolfe needs the Sarah of today to be just as bad as the Sarah of yesterday. Seeing her any other way would be like admitting she'd made a mistake, that it is possible for people to change over time. And Wolfe doesn't believe she's made any mistakes."

"Admitting Sarah has changed would also force her to face her other victims, so to speak. If Sarah could change, they all had the ability to change too."

Donna remained quiet for a minute and said, "Hey, what do you think about letting me do an interview on you? Not right now ... say, after the case is over? You have great insight into the way serial killers think and behave. We don't interview people in your line of work often. In your case though, our readers would be interested in what you have to say about Atticus Wolfe and about serial killers in general. Maybe it's time we glorify people like you instead of people like her."

Perhaps her readers would respond well to a different point of view, but I wasn't sure it was something I wanted to do. I'd chosen this life because even from a young age, it was in my blood, just as it had been in my fathers. It was like I was born to do it—to help people, to wipe the scum and filth off the streets just like he had. I suppose in my own way, I was a mission-oriented protector of the innocent.

"Let me think about the article, okay?" I asked.

"Sure, no problem. I'd have to get permission first anyway, but of course they'll say yes."

sat at the table inside my Airstream, doing some research on Trevor Armstrong's daughter Samantha—the first on my shortlist of suspects to do a little more digging into. One personal record I found came as a bit of a shock, prompting me to give Trevor a call. When I explained what I was looking at, he was hesitant to provide more details at first. He knew I saw her as a potential suspect, and he didn't want to say anything to add to those suspicions. After a fair amount of gentle persuasion on my part, I managed to convince him the best thing he could do for his daughter was to give me a reason to rule her out. He knew as well as I did if he didn't talk to me, I'd find someone else who would.

The surprising news I'd found?

Samantha was adopted.

And not as a baby, either.

She was eight years old when it happened.

Samantha entered foster care at the age of five when her mother left her sitting in a rundown restaurant with fifty dollars and a note pinned to her jacket. The note said something along the lines of, *Whoever reads this, please find a better home for my daughter than I can give her.*

Mother of the year, right there.

For three years, Samantha was bounced around from foster home to foster home until Trevor and his wife, Julie, came along. The first year after her adoption was good. Samantha had a stable home with two people she expected to be there for her for the rest of her life. Until Julie walked out, becoming the second woman in Samantha's life to abandon her.

Trevor admitted the decision to adopt Samantha all those years ago was his idea. At the time, his marriage was going south of the border, and he saw Samantha as the glue that would stick it all back together again. But kids weren't fixers. In an already unraveling relationship, Samantha was a placeholder. Trevor and Julie were the only ones with the ability to make their marriage work.

"What made you think adoption would save your marriage?" I asked.

"My wife was battling depression, had been for years. I thought Samantha would give her something to focus on, something she was missing in her life. For a while, it worked."

"And then?"

"You need to understand, Samantha was a quiet kid when she first came to us. She didn't say much, didn't make eye contact, didn't respond when we tried to talk to her. No matter how much effort my wife made, Samantha wouldn't let her in. I suppose she was still too traumatized over what had happened with her own mother to make space for any other woman in her life—even a small space."

"Makes sense."

"At the same time, Samantha's behavior toward me changed, and we started bonding. Julie saw how happy Samantha was when we were together, and she assumed it was her fault Samantha hadn't bonded with her. The guilt she put on herself was too much for Julie in the end. She walked out on us, moved back in with her parents, and filed for divorce, leaving me to raise Samantha as a single father."

"How was Samantha after Julie left?"

"Fine. Better than I thought she'd be. And look, I don't blame Julie for what she did. I blame myself. Once Julie was gone, I devoted as much of my time as I could to Samantha. I'd like to think she turned out well because of it."

Turning out well didn't mean she wasn't a killer.

The picture Trevor painted was a sad one. I was sure he believed his words would incite sympathy on my part, and they had. They also left me with a healthy-sized portion of skepticism.

"Oh, and the other night when you called, asking about Samantha. She showed up at the restaurant within fifteen minutes of your call. So, you see, it can't be her. She's innocent."

Was she?

Or was he covering for her?

Now, more than ever, I had reason to believe Samantha's regrettable past haunted her present—in more ways than one.

33

They weren't good people," Hunter said. "None of them, from everything I've learned so far."

I set the phone down on the table, put the call on speaker, and got out a notebook and pen. "I know about Sarah Peterson. She had a meth problem that resulted in a stillborn baby. What about the others?"

"Let's see, well … Jill Jacobsen, Wolfe's first victim, if you don't count her own sister, went to juvie at the age of fourteen because she beat one of her classmates with a baseball bat until he was unconscious. The next victim was Nikki Daley, who Wolfe murdered two years later. She was living a double life. Mother by day. Hooker by night. She had a habit of getting her john's drunk and then stealing money from their wallets. The rest of the women Wolfe murdered all have similar stories. Should I keep going?"

"No, it's all right. You've told me what I need to know."

"There are so many messed up people in this world, sheesh."

Hunter's tone of voice shifted, from light and informative to heavy and nervous. Cases like this were hard for her, causing her stress and anxiety. It was one of the reasons she didn't last long as a detective at the department, and it was something I paid close attention to now. The last thing I wanted was for her to become overwhelmed.

"Hey, are you okay?" I asked.

"I'm fine. I like doing this. I mean it. I just want us to solve this case before someone else dies."

"Me too. You'd tell me if anything I'm asking you to do for me is too much, right?"

She sighed. "I'm fine. You don't need to worry."

When it came to her, I would always worry. She was like a younger sister to me, someone I felt the urge to protect.

Hunter cleared her throat. "Do you have any other questions for me or is there anything else you'd like me to do?"

"Just one question for now. Wolfe's victims … what was their home life like?"

"It varied. Some grew up in middle-class, functioning families, where two parents were present. Others were raised by a single mother or father. A couple of them lived just above the poverty line and then another had a father who made a killing on Wall Street."

Nothing about their backgrounds was similar, then. It was all about who they were as people, just like Wolfe had said.

My phone beeped with another call coming in.

I looked to see who it was, then told Hunter, "I have to let you go. Okay?"

"No problem. Talk soon."

I disconnected and answered my sister's call. "Hey, Phoebe. Sorry I haven't stopped by this week. I've been preoccupied with this case. How's Lark doing? Can I come over later and see the two of—"

"Gigi," Phoebe said. "I just got home, and something weird is going on."

"What's happening?"

"There are all these sticky notes stuck to my front door with the number 1 written on them."

I pressed a hand to my chest, my heart accelerating with every passing beat. "Phoebe, where are you right now?"

"I'm on the doorstep. I'm just about to enter the house."

"Where's Lark?"

"Standing here next to me. Why? What's going on?"

"Listen to me. You're in danger. I need you to back away from the house. Do not go inside."

"Oh … kay. Are you going to tell me what's going on?"

"I will, but first, get to the edge of your driveway and let me know when you're there."

Seconds passed.

"We're here."

"Can you tell if Hattie's home, your neighbor?" I asked.

There was a pause on the line, then Phoebe said, "Yeah, she's unloading groceries from the back of her car."

"Get to Hattie's as fast as you can. Tell her I said to take you and Lark inside, lock the door, and get out her Japanese knife."

"Her Japanese *what*?"

"Trust me, Phoebe. She'll know what I mean. And don't hang up. Stay on the line with me. I'll be right there."

I grabbed the car keys and sprinted out of the Airstream, screaming for Giovanni.

34

Giovanni grabbed my hand and glanced over his shoulder, yelling for Peppe and Salvatore, his two right-hand men. We raced toward Giovanni's car and got inside, speeding through the neighborhood streets toward Phoebe's house. Giovanni stayed on the line with Phoebe, while I used his phone to call Foley to explain the potential situation. He agreed to meet us at Phoebe's house.

We parked in front of Hattie's place, and I ran inside, throwing my arms around my sister. "Are you okay? Is Lark okay? Where is she?"

"Good grief, we're fine," she said. "She's in the living room watching *The Baby-Sitters Club*."

I paused a moment to steady my breathing.

Then I shifted my focus to Hattie. "Thank you."

"Oh, you don't thank me." She thumbed in Phoebe's direction. "I'll always be here for these two. You know that."

"I do, and I appreciate it."

"Shame," Hattie said. "Every time I think I'll have an opportunity to use the knife my husband gave me, I never get the chance. What a pity."

I met Hattie a couple of years earlier when Lark had been kidnapped. She was a nosy, retired widower with too much time on her hands. While in her kitchen one day, she reached inside a drawer and pulled out one of the sharpest knives I'd ever seen. Hand-forged and made of carbon steel, it was Hattie's go-to weapon of choice whenever she suspected something was amiss in the neighborhood.

"Let's hope you never have to use it," I said.

Hattie shot me a wink. "Let's hope I do."

She meant it. I could tell.

"The new lead detective is on his way over. His name is Rex Foley. Phoebe, I need you to stay here with Hattie until the police officers clear your house."

"Then are you going to tell me what this is all about?" Phoebe asked.

If I was being honest with myself, I didn't want to tell her. Then I'd have to admit that I was the reason for the mayhem.

"I will," I said. "I'll tell you every—"

I paused midsentence.

I could have sworn I'd heard a familiar, high-pitched tone of voice. One I didn't want to hear right now.

No.

It can't be.

I grabbed Phoebe's arm. "*Please* tell me you didn't call Mom."

She took a couple of steps back.

"I mean, I don't have to tell you anything, but if it makes you feel better, I, uhh …" She bit down on her lip. "I may have texted her. I'm guessing that was a bad thing?"

I rubbed a hand along my forehead and braced for impact.

"*Yoo-hoo*, Hattie. It's me, Darlene, Phoebe's mother. Phoebe, honey, are you in here?"

Instead of waiting for someone to greet her at the door, my mother burst inside, making a beeline for Phoebe. The second she saw her, she pressed the back of her hand to her forehead like she might pass out, huffing out a dramatic, "Here you are. Thank goodness you're all right! I was so worried!"

"We're fine, Mom," Phoebe said. "I shouldn't have texted you."

"What are you talking about? You should always keep me informed of ..."

In that moment my mother realized I was there too, standing a few feet behind her. She gave me a disappointed look and folded her arms, blinking at me like she was gathering the words she wanted to say to me. Words I was sure I didn't need to hear right now. Not wanting to stick around and wait for her to unload another lecture on me, I headed outside and found Giovanni and Harvey in a conversation with Foley.

Great.

Just great.

First my mother.

Now this.

I glanced across Phoebe's front yard, looking to see if Blackwell was hovering around somewhere too. I didn't see him, which meant one of two things. He was either inside Phoebe's house, or he wasn't around at all.

I prayed it was the latter.

Foley saw me and broke from the conversation. He approached me and said, "Germaine, I just met your, uhh, well ... your ... you know, I'm not sure what he is to you. He didn't say."

"We live together."

We *live* together?

I'd made it sound like we were roommates.

"He's my boyfriend," I clarified. "Where is Blackwell? I thought he'd be here."

"He's, ahh, following up on something else right now."

His cryptic answer spoke volumes.

Where was that guy?

Whatever Blackwell was doing had to have been important, or he would have been here.

"How's the sweep of the house going?" I asked.

"Officers Higgins and Decker are going through your sister's place now. We'll see what they find."

"This is the second message the killer has left me in twenty-four hours, as you know."

"Any idea why?"

"I must be getting close to discovering her identity."

"You think so?"

I knew so.

I wanted to probe more into the fact Blackwell was absent without it being obvious, so I said, "What about you? What's happening on your end? Any new leads?"

He kicked some loose gravel with his foot, staring across the street at nothing in particular. "Information is trickling in here and there."

Still aloof.

I got to the point.

"What aren't you telling me?" I asked.

"What aren't *you* telling *me*?"

Plenty.

But nothing of major significance.

"If there was something you needed to know, something like this for example, I'd tell you," I said.

He sighed. "You understand my position, right?"

"If by *position* you mean Blackwell expecting you not to share anything with me, then yes, I do."

He was about to respond when Officer Higgins walked out of Phoebe's house. As he headed our way, I could see he was carrying a couple of items in his hands. Items I didn't recognize at first. When they came into view, I gasped. If this was the killer's idea of getting my attention, she had it.

35

Foley exchanged glances with Higgins and said, "It's a bit too early in the evening, don't you think?"

It was an ill-timed quip to try and lighten the mood, and a comment neither Higgins nor I found amusing. It didn't take long for Foley to realize his comedic failure and stop talking.

Higgins raised his hands, showing Foley the contents of the plastic bags. "Found this bottle of wine in the kitchen along with a business card."

"What's on the card?" Foley asked.

Higgins glanced at me and frowned.

"Don't look at her," Foley said. "Look at me."

"I need to ask her a question."

"Whatever it is, it can wait. What's on the business card?"

"It's just … we know from the other two crime scenes that the Holliday sisters were poisoned. This bottle of wine could have been left by the killer, or it could have been left by you, Germaine."

By me?

What was he talking about?

And why was he dancing around the contents of the note?

"What's going on, Higgins?" I asked.

"Did you leave a bottle of wine in your sister's kitchen?"

I shook my head. "I haven't been here all week. Why?"

"The business card I found next to the bottle indicates the wine is from you."

"Well, it's not. Was it a handwritten note?"

"Typed and then stuck to the back of the card."

Clever girl.

"Are you going to tell us what's on the business card in this millennia?" Foley asked. "Or do I need to rip open the bag and see it for myself?"

"There's not much to it," Higgins said.

Foley snatched the baggie from Higgins' hand and inspected it. I leaned over to get a better look myself. Inside the baggie was a business card—*my* business card. Foley flipped the baggie over. On the back of the card, it said: *Thought you'd enjoy this! – Georgiana*

"First off, I would never sign it with my entire name," I said. "Phoebe calls me Gigi. She has ever since we were kids."

"Who have you given your business card to lately?" Foley asked.

Anyone and everyone.

"Every single person I've talked to about this case."

"I'll need a list of names—today."

"It will be most of the same people you've interviewed about the case too."

Foley shoved the business card back inside the baggie and handed it to Higgins. "Get this stuff to Silas for processing. And I want an officer assigned to this house starting now, understand?"

"We already have two men posted at Alli Kane's house," Higgins said. "We're going to run out of officers to assign."

"I didn't ask you for your opinion, Higgins," Foley said. "I told you what I wanted you to do. Now do it, or you can explain to Blackwell why we weren't here when the perp returned to finish the job."

Higgins heaved a frustrated sigh. "Yeah, fine. I'll see what I can do."

"You won't *see* anything. You'll make it happen—tonight."

As Higgins stormed off, I thought about Foley's decision to park an officer in front of my sister's house. I knew every officer at the department, and I trusted them. They were great guys. Guys who could be counted on. But I wasn't leaving her here.

"You don't need to worry about sparing any more of your men," I said. "I'm taking my sister and my niece to my place."

"And if your sister doesn't want to go?"

"She doesn't have a choice. She's going."

He tugged at his chin. "Don't blame you, I suppose. If it was my sister, I'd do the same thing."

"All I've ever wanted is to keep my family safe. This is all happening because of me."

"Don't be too hard on yourself. It's part of the job. It always has been. You know the risks."

The risks felt a lot different when it hit this close to home.

The killer had my attention. If she hoped to survive long enough to see life through the steel bars of her cell … well, maybe she should have thought about that before she went after *my* sister. She'd made it personal, and I couldn't wait for the opportunity to return the favor.

As the rage within me brimmed to the surface, Foley tipped his head toward Giovanni's car and said, "Those guys sitting in the back seat of the Rolls-Royce … who are they?"

I glanced over my shoulder at Peppe and Salvatore, thinking about how to explain them to him—or anyone. The look on Foley's face said he already knew. He was just curious about what I'd say.

"They work for Giovanni," I said.

"Doing what?"

"Does it matter?"

"That car alone is worth, what—three, four hundred thousand?"

"I don't know. I've never bothered to ask."

Hattie's screen door opened, and Phoebe walked out. I waved her over.

"Did they find anything?" she asked.

"A couple of things. They've taken some items into evidence."

"You're saying someone was inside my house?"

"I am."

Now wasn't the right moment to bring up how many times I'd asked her to install a security system. Maybe now she'd take me seriously.

Phoebe ran her hands along her arms. "Gives me chills thinking about it."

"I know, and I'm sorry. Let's go pack some of your things, and you and Lark can come stay with me for a while."

"Is that necessary? Are we in danger?"

"Not if you're with us," I said. "We'll keep the two of you safe."

"I don't understand. Why is this happening, Gigi?"

She stared at me with her big doe eyes. I considered putting her off again. But she wanted answers, and I had to be the one to give them to her.

"I was hired by Greer Holliday to investigate her sister's murder," I said. "The same week she hired me, Greer was murdered too. The killer is aware I'm tracking her. She's started leaving me messages … this time, through you. There was a bottle of wine left on your kitchen counter with a business card. The note on the back of the card says it's from me. It isn't. There's a lot more I need to tell you, but for right now, let's focus on getting you both out of here. Once we're at my place, you can ask me anything you want."

Foley cleared his throat loud enough for it to be heard all the way down the street.

"Oh yeah," I said. "Phoebe, this is the detective I was telling you about."

He extended a hand toward her. "Detective Rex Foley. If there's anything you need, you let me know. I'll make sure you have my details before you leave."

Anything she needs?

And why is he staring at her like an infatuated puppy?

"I ... uhh, thanks," Phoebe said.

She curled a lock of hair over her ear and bit down on her lip, something she did when she was feeling coy, and her cheeks were a lot redder than usual.

Foley smiled at her.

She smiled at him.

I didn't like it.

I didn't like it at all.

"Seems like you've got everything all wrapped up here, Foley," I said. "I'm sure there are other places you need to be."

He snapped out of his smitten haze and nodded.

"Yep. You're right. Blackwell's waiting on me. I should go."

Yes, you should.

The sooner the better.

He reached into his pocket, opened his wallet, and handed Phoebe one of his cards. "I meant what I said. Call me anytime."

Foley walked toward his car, and Phoebe's eyes stayed on him. As he pulled onto the street, she turned toward me. I knew what she was about to ask.

"Yes, he's single," I said. "At least, I think he is. But if he's anything like the racist creep he works for, you might want to keep your distance." I slung an arm around her, and we walked toward the house. "There's so much we need to catch up on. This new case

I've been working has me thinking about us. I know we don't see each other as much as we should, and I'm sorry."

"Oh, stop it. We're both busy."

It wasn't just about being busy. It was about opening up to each other the way we used to, the way we did before Fallon died. I still had a long way to go to get back to the woman I wanted to be.

Awareness was the first step of any lasting change, a closed door cracking open. Little by little, it inched me forward. I had enough self-awareness to know I'd never feel whole again, not without my daughter. That chunk had been carved out of me the moment she left this life. Now all I could do was focus on the part of me that remained—the part that kept me in the land of the living. Friends, family … love.

We spent the next hour layering items in bags to be taken to my place. Phoebe still wasn't keen on the idea, but Lark bounced around the house like we were all headed to Disneyland. And I had to admit, part of me felt giddy knowing we'd get some extra time together.

Once we were all packed, Giovanni took one of the duffel bags out of my hands, and I walked with him toward the car. The emotions I had about the attempt on my sister's life were weighing on me. I wanted to confide in him, but I worried if I did, I might burst into a tirade of fury and tears.

We set the bags in the trunk, and he wrapped his arms around me. "Whatever you need from me, just ask."

I shelved the urge to act like I could handle things myself and said, "I want Peppe and Salvatore to keep an eye on Phoebe and Lark when I can't, just until this case is over."

"Of course."

I leaned in for a quick kiss. "Thank you."

"And if she returns—the woman you're after? What would you have them do?"

It was a loaded question, with a simple answer: whatever it took to spare the lives of two people who meant everything to me.

For as much as I'd changed since my daughter died, and all the effort I'd gone through to reconcile my past, the thought that this woman was out there, trying to get inside my head at the expense of my own family had stirred something up in me. Something dark and vengeful. Something that wanted to strike back and strike hard.

A few nights ago, when Giovanni told me he'd do anything for his family, I'd thought we were different. I thought my family didn't require the same sacrifice his did. I was wrong. We were much more alike than I realized, and for the first time, I felt I could admit what I wanted.

"If she comes back, if she *dares* come for my sister again, or me, or anyone I love … tell them to shoot her."

36

After Phoebe and Lark went off to bed, I sat with Giovanni—after pouring myself a glass of wine from a bottle I was sure hadn't been tampered with today. Given the number of security cameras around the place, no one was getting in and out of our home without us knowing about it. Still, I couldn't help but have a slight hesitation as I took my first sip.

"Something occurred to me when we were at Phoebe's place," I said. "I was unfair to you the other night."

He set his glass on the table and rested a hand on my leg. "What do you mean?"

"I've always assumed your views on family differed from mine. Now I know I was wrong. When Higgins walked out of my sister's house and I saw the wine bottle in the evidence bag, all I could think about was what I would have done if I lost my sister tonight."

"Did you come up with an answer?"

"I did. As much as I want to believe I'd never take another person's life, tonight I realized no matter how much I believe in the justice system, even I have a breaking point."

He tipped his head to the side, staring at me for a time. I wondered what might be going on inside his head. Had what I said caused him to see me in a different light? Didn't matter. I was glad I said it. If we didn't have honesty, we had nothing.

"I hope you never know what it's like to end another's life, cara mia, even if you believe you're justified in doing so. It sits in the pit of your stomach, festering like a cancer as it spreads. Always there. Always reminding you of what you've done. Reminding you of the life you took—someone's father, brother, son."

"If you feel that way, why have you done it?"

"When Lark was kidnapped," he said, "you found the man who took her. You brought him to justice. He was sent to prison, as he should have been."

Anthony Paine had gone to prison, though he didn't last long. Within months, he met his end when a fellow inmate slit his throat while Anthony was eating his morning bowl of oatmeal.

"Justice may have prevailed in the eyes of the court, but all his fellow inmates saw was a man who'd abducted an innocent child," I said.

"You're right. And no matter what Anthony said or didn't say in his defense, it didn't matter. The men he was locked up with had already decided what they wanted to do with him. There was nothing he could have said to save himself."

I sipped my wine and thought about that for a long moment. "I remember meeting with Anthony after he was arrested, listening as he told me his story. As he explained why he did what he did, I wanted to feel something for him—sympathy, concern, anything. I felt nothing. He'd killed Lark's father right in front of her, robbing her of the innocent childhood she deserved. She was still in therapy, and although she was recovering somewhat, we all knew she would never be the same again."

"The justice system today is sometimes fair, sometimes flawed, and sometimes not the right fit for every situation," he said. "It may work for most families. It doesn't work for mine."

In Giovanni's family there was expectation, rules meant to be followed. Break them and there was no need to call the authorities. The family took care of problems their own way, as they had ever since Salvatore Maranzano established the American mob in the 1930s.

My cell phone sounded off, and I glanced at the time. It was just after eleven at night, an unusual time to receive a call. I looked at the caller ID and then answered it.

"Silas, is everything all right?"

"Hey, this is … first chance I've … call you."

"You're cutting out. I can't hear everything you're saying."

"Hold on."

I heard what sounded like someone rushing around, followed by a door slamming.

"Okay, I'm outside. Is this better? You there?"

"I'm here. What's up?"

"I just arrived at the lab.

"Why are you working so late at night?"

"It's happened again."

"What's happened?"

"There's been another murder."

37

Another murder. The killer was one busy bee, hitting two houses in the same day. For a second, I wondered if she wasn't working alone. But other than her ability to multitask, I had no reason to indulge that theory—yet.

I thought back to what Foley had said earlier when I asked about Blackwell and was told he was following up on something else. Silas had been notified about the murder just after five p.m., after the victim's husband called the police. It meant Foley learned of the murder while we were at my sister's house and hadn't told me. I didn't blame him. If it were me, and he was the private investigator, I wouldn't have told him either.

The victim's name was Naomi Collins. She was twenty-eight years old, one year older than Pippa and one year younger than Greer. It couldn't have been a coincidence. She had a six-month-old daughter and was married to Ben, a pharmacist she'd met and married while in college.

Naomi lived in Cayucos, a short twenty-minute drive from my sister's place, making it easy for the killer to get from one place to the other in the same day.

Naomi's body had been staged like the others. A bottle of wine wasn't found, but according to the husband, Naomi didn't drink—not wine anyway. Her addiction of choice was soda, and a half-empty can was discovered on the coffee table in the living room, right next to her lifeless body.

This time, a child wasn't around at the time of the murder. Ben had taken the baby with him to the grocery store, leaving Naomi all alone.

One minute, he was kissing his wife, promising to return soon.

The next, his wife was dead.

Life was fleeting—too fleeting sometimes.

Tonight, the Collins household was crawling with members of the police department, making the house and a conversation with Ben off-limits for now.

I slipped into bed, snuggled next to Giovanni, and drifted off to sleep thinking of the latest victim.

Who was she?

And what was her connection to the Holliday sisters?

38

"Well, well. Look who it is. You figure your case out yet? I'm guessing you haven't. Otherwise, you wouldn't be here."

Once again, I found myself sitting across from Wolfe. Not wanting to stroke her ego, I'd debated whether seeing her again was the right choice. But with last night's murder, I figured it was worth a second visit.

While I talked to Wolfe, Hunter was busy digging up whatever dirt she could find on Naomi Collins. I wanted to know who she was, how the murders were connected. What I wanted more than anything was to discover the killer's motive. I was close. So close. I could feel it.

"The other day, you made reference to a hexagon, a shape that leaves no wasted space," I said. "And then there was the message you asked Blackwell to give me about the wolf seeing shapes and shadows. They're clues, aren't they?"

A wry grin spread across Wolfe's face. "Putting two and two together, are we?"

"How about six—the number of sides on a hexagon?"

"And what would be the significance of such a number?"

"The woman I'm after ... she killed again last night, right after an attempt on my sister's life. A wine bottle was left at her house, along with a message from me—only it wasn't from me."

"Are you certain the wine was poisoned?"

"Why wouldn't it be?"

"And you think your sister's part of the pattern, part of, what shall we call it? How about the Slick Six?"

"My sister's not part of the pattern, if there is one. She was the means to an end—a message from the killer to me. Nothing more."

Wolfe leaned back and nodded, looking pleased, like I just earned my first gold star, and she was the teacher taking all the credit. "What message do you believe the killer's sending you?"

"She's someone I've met before, someone I've questioned."

"And yet you still don't know who."

"I have my suspicions."

"Care to share?"

I didn't.

But I did say, "She's made contact with you somehow since you've been in prison."

"I've had few visitors over the years, as you're aware."

"I'm not talking about visitors. I'm talking about all forms of correspondence—letters in particular."

She blinked several times, working extra hard to keep her expression from changing. But it *had* changed, a slight, but noticeable crack in her perfect, impenetrable varnish.

Come on, Wolfe.

Crack.

Let's see it.

She closed her eyes for a moment and took in a deep breath, as if centering herself as she readied her response. "Any letters we receive are opened by mailroom staff."

Nice try.

"Opened, yes. Read? Not always. Staff looks at every photograph. They search for contraband. But do they pore over every word or recognize a pattern or a hidden code when they see one? The answer is no. Not often."

"Getting warmer, I must say. Continue."

"I talked to the warden about your time here. You've been a model prisoner for decades. You've kept yourself out of trouble and have never harmed anyone, which must have been hard. You've even managed to get on the good side of several of the guards here. You could have been corresponding with the person I'm after for years, and no one suspected a thing."

"You seem so sure of yourself today. More like your father."

I wasn't here to take another trip down memory lane.

I was here for answers.

"The last time I was here to talk to you, I asked the warden to provide me with a list of every person who's written you since your incarceration. They keep track, as you know. He chose not to give it to me and offered it to Blackwell instead. Now that there has been a third murder, it seems he's had a change of heart."

She shrugged. "Good for him."

"Three murders down, three to go—right?"

"Take all the time you need going over your little list from the warden. Things aren't always what they seem."

"You're suggesting she wrote you under an alias, a fake name, so nothing could connect back to her."

"I haven't suggested any such thing."

But she had.

"How long do I have until she strikes again?" I asked.

"Oh, I couldn't tell you that."

"Why are you protecting her?"

She narrowed her eyes. "I'm not."

"Then tell me who she is."

"I'll leave the detective work to you, if you don't mind."

I slammed my fist onto the table. "I do mind! More women are going to die. I need to stop her before she kills again."

"If more women die at her hand, they deserve what's coming to them. If you can't stop her, then I suppose you'll have to live with the knowledge they died on your watch … because you weren't good enough at your job. You can't even see what's right in front of your face."

I wanted to yank every hair from her nasty head and shove it down her throat, and judging by the way she was glaring at me, she knew it.

"What did they do to her—Pippa and Greer and Naomi?" I asked. "What did they do to make her so angry she wanted them all dead?"

"Excellent question. Now run along and find the answer. Better hurry." Wolfe glanced up at one of the guards. "I'm ready to go now."

I sat there wondering what to say in our final moments together, and then it came to me. "I *will* find her, and when I do, this thing between the two of you will come to an end. You'll grow even older and more pitiful than you already are, and you'll die here, alone, because not a single person cares enough about you to attend your funeral."

Wolfe looked me in the eye, smiling as she said, "I wasn't sure you had it in you. Bravo, Germaine. Bravo."

39

As I made my way out of the prison, I passed a room full of female inmates who appeared to be taking a cooking class. A placard on the front of the closed door read: *Anna St. James Culinary Academy*. The last time I visited, the room had been vacant, the lights off. Just another empty, nondescript room—one of many in this place. Now I could see it served as much more.

I looked over at the guard serving as my escort. "I didn't know there were programs like this in here."

Without looking at me, he grunted, "Some."

Man of few words.

"Has it been here long?"

"It's new. Well, new*ish*."

"The women seem to like it."

"Guess so."

And with that, the conversation came to an abrupt halt.

"I'm supposed to see the warden before I leave," I said.

He nodded, and we continued in silence. When we arrived at Warden Jackson's office, the guard made an abrupt turn, leaving me there as he headed in the opposite direction.

I rapped on the door and heard, "What is it?"

"It's Georgiana Germaine. Stopping by to get the list of names of all people who've corresponded with Wolfe over the years."

"Come on in."

Warden Jackson tugged on his thick, gray moustache and asked me to take a seat. He pushed a pair of square-framed glasses higher up on his nose, opened a drawer, pulled out a file folder, and handed me a small stack of papers. "You asked for all the names of people who wrote to her since her incarceration. I'm giving you everyone from the last year."

"And the previous years?"

"Take what you can get and be grateful for it."

It seemed I didn't have a choice.

"Thanks for letting me see her again," I said.

"Don't thank me. If she hadn't agreed to it, you wouldn't be here. How'd it go, anyway?"

"She knows something about the murders and who's committing them."

He laced his hands behind his head. "You sure she's not just yanking your chain?"

"I'm sure."

"I don't know what to say. We could talk to her. Not sure how far we'd get."

"Nowhere, I'm guessing," I said. "She's enjoying the view from the cheap seats, waiting to see if the case gets solved before the next murder. Has she had any visitors since I was here last?"

He shook his head.

It wasn't what I hoped, but it was what I expected.

"The new culinary academy is nice," I said.

"Sure is. A lot of the gals here love it. Gives them a skill, something to look forward to each day. Food's been a lot better around here too."

"How long has it been running?" I asked.

"Oh, a handful of years, or so. Had an inmate here for a while charged with manslaughter. Sad story. Ran over a teenager one night after she'd been drinking at some fancy schmancy rich guy's party. Kid died before they could get him to the hospital. She cried every night for the first three months straight. Had her on suicide watch for a long while."

"The inmate is no longer here, then?"

He shook his head. "No, ma'am. She served her time and was released a few years back. After she got out, she wanted to do something for her fellow inmates. She'd made friends with many of them, and she knew some would never get out of here. She offered to pay for the culinary center, and we thought it was a great idea."

"This woman … Anna St. James. She wouldn't happen to be related to Laney St. James, the actress?"

He leaned forward, crossing his arms over the desk. "Sure is. She's Laney's older sister."

40

"Open up, Laney. I know you're in there."

For the last few minutes, I'd been standing on her porch, pounding on the door, while the security camera swiveled back and forth overhead.

She was in there.

And she was watching me.

Or someone was, at least.

I felt stupid for ruling her out as a suspect, throwing her back to sea. Waiting outside of her house now, I was desperate to reel her back in. And this time, she'd have to do a hell of a lot more to convince me she wasn't behind the murders. The connection to Pippa and Greer was there.

Was it also there with Naomi Collins?

The door cracked open, and she peeked out. "You said never to contact you again."

"That was *before* I learned your sister was in prison with Atticus Wolfe. "

"Who's Atticus Wolfe?"

"Don't act like you don't know."

"You need to leave. Get off my property. I have nothing to say to you."

She attempted to slam the door, and I kicked my foot into the doorway, stopping her.

"What is your freaking deal!" she shrieked. "Get out of here!"

I leaned the full force of my weight against the door and shoved my way inside. The martini she was holding flew out of her hand, shattering along the floor.

Laney surveyed the damage and said, "That's it. I'm calling the police."

She grabbed her cell phone out of her pocket, and I snatched it. "I'm not going anywhere until we talk."

"Oh, yes you are."

She attempted to flee, and I grabbed her wrist.

"Ow! You're hurting me!"

"Three women are dead, Laney," I said. "Three! Either you prove to me right now that you're not responsible, or I'll take you to see the police myself."

She rested her forehead against the wall and began sobbing, an emotion I hadn't expected.

Was she acting?

Or were her tears genuine?

"You're such an asshole," she spouted. "Do you realize what I'm going through right now? The man I love isn't leaving his wife, and here you are, *again*, accusing me of murders I didn't commit."

"All you need to do is prove you're innocent, and I'll leave."

"The cops have already been here, multiple times, and detectives, and everyone else. They know all about my sister. I've been cleared."

"You have?"

She sniffled a few times and nodded.

"When were they here?" I asked.

"A couple of days ago."

I released her wrist and handed her cell phone back. "I believed you were innocent too, and then this morning, I found out about your sister. I was sure it was the connection I was missing."

"You're wrong, okay? It wasn't me. Look, I heard about this new girl who died last night, this Naomi whatever. I was in a meeting with the production company for my next film yesterday for most of the day. I didn't head home until after dark. I can give you the producer's name if you want, and she'll tell you. The news said this Naomi woman died in Cayucos. It's at least a three-hour drive from here. You see how it's impossible the person you're looking for is me, right?"

"I ... yeah, I do."

"And since the cops already asked and I know you're going to ask too, my sister had nothing to do with the murders either. She's in London. And yes, the detective who was here confirmed that too. She hasn't traveled back to the States in over six months. It's not her, and it's not me."

I felt two-inches tall.

Maybe even one inch.

I wished I could slip through the cracks in the floor and disappear, or better yet, push a rewind button that would allow me to go about this in a different way, a better way. I'd been so hung up on the new information I'd found out and the fact she'd refused to come to the door when I arrived, I convinced myself it was her—she was the villain in this twisted story.

"Look, Laney, I'm sorry. I shouldn't have—"

"Judged me? You're right. You shouldn't have. But you did. You and everyone else. I shouldn't be surprised. I'm used to it."

"I wouldn't blame you if you wanted to slap me across the face right now."

She cracked a slight smile. "Is that an invitation?"

"I'm sure you don't want to talk to me after what just happened, but I was hoping I could ask you a few more things about Pippa. I'm starting to think she wasn't the person I thought she was when I first took this case."

"Took you long enough." She took a few steps back. "I tell ya what. I'll answer your question *if* you let me slap you across the face."

I considered the offer.

I'd had worse.

I stepped forward.

"Go ahead," I said. "Do it."

She whipped her hand back and thrust it forward, stopping so close to my face I felt a burst of air brush across my cheek. Then she tossed her head back, snorting a devious laugh. She swirled her finger at me and said, "I'm starting to think you're even crazier than I am, and that's saying something."

She had no idea.

"Rude of you to ruin my drink, by the way," she said.

"Yeah, I'm sorry about that too."

"You should be. The martini glass you just shattered was a Waterford. It's worth a hundred bucks."

"I'll pay for it."

"Don't worry about it. I would like to make another drink though. You want one?"

"No thanks."

"Suit yourself. You're missing out."

Laney walked to a gold bar cart with marble shelving. She grabbed a bottle of vodka and vermouth. Then we proceeded to the kitchen, and she opened the refrigerator, pulling out a small container of olives. She showed it to me and said, "You ever have a dirty martini with Parmigiano cream-stuffed olives?"

I hadn't.

She tapped a fingernail to the bottle. "These beauties are imported from Italy. Best olives I've ever had. They make the drink. Well, most of it."

"What are all those trays in your refrigerator?"

She turned back. "Makeup."

"I had no idea people kept makeup in the fridge."

"It's not your run-of-the-mill, average-person stuff. It's expensive. More expensive than most people can afford."

Perhaps it was time to up my cosmetics game.

She fixed herself a cocktail and sat next to me. "You said you had questions. What are they?"

"I wanted to ask you about Samantha Armstrong."

"I don't have any idea who you're talking about."

"Trevor Armstrong was Pippa's boyfriend. Samantha is his daughter. You never saw her on set?"

"If she was, it wasn't when I was there. Pippa never liked talking about her personal life. Not to me, anyway."

"What did you think of Pippa's relationship with her sister?"

She took a sip of her martini. "Greer was a real piece of work. She liked to be involved in all aspects of Pippa's life. I never understood why Pippa didn't stand up to her, but she didn't. Maybe it was an older sister, younger sister thing. Whatever it was, I didn't get it."

"How was Greer controlling?"

"Whenever she was on set, she inserted her unsolicited advice into everything Pippa did. She was always looking over her shoulder. Wherever Pippa was, Greer was right beside her."

I thought back to Pippa's dinner party. According to Greer, she'd helped Pippa set up and then left. If she always wanted to be by her sister's side, why hadn't she stayed that night?

"Remember the last time I was here, and you told me Donovan Grant gave you a call after he left Pippa's party and told you the party was a snorefest?"

"Yeah."

"What else did he say about it? I'm asking because I find it odd that Greer didn't stay for the party."

"Oh, I'll tell you why. Donovan told me Pippa and Greer got into an argument at the start of the party. Then Greer went home."

"What was the argument about?"

She swirled the olive-covered toothpick around her drink and took a bite.

"He didn't know. He was outside with the other guests and saw Pippa and Greer going at it inside the house. Pippa wouldn't say what happened, but Donovan said Pippa was quieter than usual the rest of the night."

"You know where I can find Donovan Grant?"

She raised a brow, eyeing me like she wasn't sure whether she should tell me or not.

"I'll find him, either way," I said. "Or you could make it easy on me and just tell me. I want to ask him about the night Pippa died."

"Mmm, all right. Sure he won't mind. Augustus Villas on Elm Court, 38b. You didn't hear it from me. Got it?"

I was shocked she'd given in after the way I'd behaved.

"Why are you helping me?"

She cocked her head to one side. "I dunno. Guess I've had a lot on my mind since Pippa died. When I said she was a snake in the grass, I suppose it was a harsh thing to say."

"Why the change of heart?"

"In all honesty, I know she didn't *take* my job from me, and I was jealous. One day she was a C-list actress, the next she was handed everything I'd worked so hard to achieve."

"I can understand why it would be upsetting."

"It was more than upsetting. It was a dagger through my heart. But it wasn't her fault. As soon as she got the news, the first thing she did was come talk to me about it."

"What did she say?"

"She wanted to tell me before I heard it from anyone else. I flipped out, of course. I shouldn't have. Do you want to know something? She sent me flowers every week while I was in rehab."

"Sounds like you're admitting she was a good person."

"I'm saying she didn't deserve to die. I hope you find out who murdered her."

"I will." I glanced at my watch. "I better be going. Thanks again."

She walked me to the door.

As I stepped onto the porch, she said, "Oh, and one more thing."

"Yeah?"

She grinned. "Don't ever contact me again."

Cheeky.

And I deserved it.

41

D onovan Grant?"

Donovan stepped into the hallway and glanced in both directions, even though it was just the two of us. "I'm curious … how did you manage to get past security?"

Wouldn't you like to know?

"I have my ways," I said.

"Is that so. And you are?"

"A private detective. My name's Georgiana Germaine."

"I suppose you're here about Pippa, just like everyone else."

"I am. Can you spare a few minutes?"

"I could …"

He just hadn't decided if he wanted to, yet. Eyes narrow, he held my gaze for a time and then pulled the door open and headed in the other direction, glancing back to say, "Are you coming in, or what?"

I followed him to a living room, stopping to check out the sweeping panoramic view of Los Angeles through the large picture windows.

"Wow, great view of the city," I said.

"My wife's a sucker for a nice view, even if it means we paid too much for this place." He gestured toward one of two black leather sofas facing each other in the living room. "Take a seat. You have ten minutes. I have a tee time to get to, and I won't be late."

For a man in his sixties, Donovan was a handsome fellow, with eyes so blue, it was hard to focus on anything else. His thick, salt-and-pepper hair had a slight curl to it, and to top it all off, he smelled like bergamot and patchouli and spoke with a heady British accent.

Ten minutes wasn't long enough.

"You acted alongside Pippa in *A Murderous Affair*."

"Yes, I played her father. Have you seen the show?"

After taking the case, I'd binge-watched both seasons, skimming through and stopping at the good bits. It held my interest, and few shows did.

"I've seen it."

"And?"

"It's good," I said.

"What do you like about it?"

I was starting to feel like I was the one being interviewed.

"It's not predictable."

"And?"

Geez, dude. What do you want from me?

If I was going to get anywhere with him, it was clear his ego needed to be stroked first.

"The love triangle between you and the two women you're trying to choose between is intriguing. One episode I'm rooting for Rita. The next, Jean."

He cupped a hand to the side of his mouth and whispered, "I hope it's Jean."

I cupped a hand to the side of mine and answered, "Me too."

"What can I do for you, Detective?"

"The night Pippa was murdered you saw her arguing with her sister in the kitchen. Do you know what the disagreement was about?"

"No, I don't. None of us did. I will say this—at times Pippa and Greer had a complicated relationship."

"Complicated how?"

"I don't know much about Pippa's personal life, but a few times on set, when we were waiting to film a scene, she opened up about it."

"What did she say?"

"Her parents were overachieving workaholics. Both doctors. Both married to their work. Since they weren't around much, Greer became almost like a mother figure, instead of a sister. Pippa always seemed to be going out of her way to please her. It wasn't the healthiest of relationships."

"What did you think of Greer?"

"We got along fine, though I didn't like how she treated Pippa sometimes."

"Can you give me an example?"

He leaned forward, clenching his hands together. "Sure, yeah. There was this one night when we were all supposed to go for a drink after we finished filming. Pippa told Greer she was going out with a bunch of us, and Greer was upset that Pippa didn't invite her along."

"Why didn't she?"

"I imagine she wanted a breather, some time to herself. Anyway, Greer threw a huge fit and walked off. Pippa chased after her, and a few minutes later, Pippa returned to say she wasn't going. She'd decided to get a late-night snack with Greer instead."

"Sounds manipulative on Greer's part."

"Greer knew what to say and how to act to get what she wanted. I think Pippa started to realize it before she died. She told me she was dating someone who'd suggested she start standing up for herself, thinking for herself. Someone who was trying to get her to step out of her sister's shadow."

"Are you talking about Trevor Armstrong?"

"Think so, yeah."

"Did you know she was hiding their relationship from Greer?"

He nodded.

"Did you ever see Pippa stand up to her sister?"

"A few times. In small ways, at first, and then she got a bit bolder."

"Bolder, how?"

"The house she purchased in Cambria ... Greer tried talking her out of buying it numerous times, but Pippa held firm. I think Greer had some fantasy of them buying a house together—using Pippa's money, of course."

Sheesh.

Working together day in and day out wasn't enough?

Donovan continued. "Greer lived her life through her sister. We could all see it. When Pippa started realizing it for herself, she told me she was buying a place somewhere outside of Hollywood, where she could go and unwind. She knew the subdivision was too rich for Greer's blood, which was also a great selling point, I expect. The closest thing Greer could find was several miles away."

He slapped a hand to his leg and stood. "Bloody nice to meet you, but I'm afraid our time has come to an end."

We took the elevator downstairs and parted ways. As his car was brought around and he drove away, I couldn't stop thinking about Greer. The more I learned about her, the more I wondered if Pippa was an innocent victim, a woman who got caught up in her sister's mess. If she had, she'd paid the ultimate price for it.

42

Hunter gathered intel on our third victim, Naomi Collins, in record time. Though it wasn't difficult. The chick's life story was splashed all over her Facebook page for everyone to see.

No privacy settings.

No social awareness.

No consideration to the reality that she'd been giving out her daily routine to anyone and everyone interested in viewing it.

Morning selfies consisted of her posing with her protein smoothie of the day. Sometimes she posted a photo. Other times a video, telling how you, dear follower, in a few easy steps, could make the same one too. Smoothie photos were followed by candid shots she took throughout the day at her job as a professional photographer. Around three, she had an afternoon latte. At four, she hit the gym. By five, she was home in time to relieve the nanny and start posting photo after photo of her precious baby.

The "about" section of Naomi's bio listed her as a photographer living in Cayucos. She was from Pismo Beach, about an hour's drive from Cambria. She attended high school at Jefferson High and college at a tech school in San Luis Obispo. In the "contact" section, I found links to her website and Instagram pages. I learned she listened to Fall Out Boy, Eminem, and Luke Bryan. Her favorite movie was *Silver Linings Playbook*.

And she liked to post quotes.

Lots and lots of quotes.

Her Instagram page was littered with them, quote after quote about living your best life, being happy, letting that shit go …

Go your way, embrace life, forget the past, there's nothing for you there.
Find peace with yourself and move forward.
Don't waste time pushing through smoke only to get to a dirty mirror.
Destiny awaits, what are you waiting for.

Blah.

Blah.

Unsolicited advice blah.

Sitting in bed with my laptop open in front of me, I stared at the last photo Naomi had taken of herself before she was murdered, I wondered who she *really* was—the woman hiding behind the wide smile and perfect teeth. To an outsider looking in, her life had revolved around promoting the ideal that "you too could be this happy" *if* you drank smoothies, and worked out, and said your morning mantras enough times.

No one was this perfect.

Were they?

Maybe they were, and I was the one with the problem.

Or maybe I needed to start lapping up the Kool-Aid, too.

I moved on to Pippa and Greer's social media presence. A search of Pippa's website didn't reveal much, and if Greer had a personal social media page, it was hidden from view. A Google search on Pippa landed me on her Wikipedia page. In the "early life" section I found not only my best clue yet, but the link that connected all three victims—Jefferson High School.

And the answers I needed now couldn't wait until morning.

43

Alli Kane gave me a puzzled, unenthusiastic look when I arrived on her doorstep. "Detective Germaine? It's a little late for visitors. What are you doing here?"

"How's Cooper doing?" I asked.

"The same. It's taken a few days, but he's started warming up to my mother, talking to us a little more."

"How long is she planning on staying here?"

"I don't know. As long as I need her to, I guess."

I glanced over my shoulder. "It's good to see the police are still hanging around."

She rolled her eyes. "If you say so. I'm guessing you didn't drive over this late at night to talk about Cooper or the cops. Why are you here?"

"I'm here because you lied to me."

She took a step back, feigned a look of shock. "Excuse me?"

"Last time I came by, I asked if you knew why Pippa told her boyfriend she regretted something from her past. You said you didn't."

She moved a hand to her hip. "Because I don't."

"Have you seen the news today?"

"We've avoided putting the news on ever since Cooper got here. We're worried he might see something about his mom. Why?"

"There was another murder last night."

She shrugged. "Bummer."

Bummer?

Her lack of sympathy was telling.

"Care to know the name of the victim?" I asked.

"Sure, why not?"

"Naomi Collins."

"Never heard of her."

"I'm guessing it's because Collins was her married name. Her maiden name is Naomi Olsen. Ring a bell now?"

Alli's eyes widened.

And the memory returns …

"I can't believe it," she stammered. "I don't understand."

"The thing is, I think you *do* understand, and you'd better start talking, because right now the one person I can connect to all three murders is you. Before Pippa died, she was having regrets about her past. I believe you know what those regrets were."

She exhaled a nervous sigh and bowed her head. Whether the sigh was one of guilt or innocence, I couldn't decide. "It can't be a coincidence."

"What can't be a coincidence?"

Alli folded her arms, refusing to answer my question.

I pulled my cell phone out of my pocket. "I have Detective Foley on speed-dial. Perhaps I should give him a call, and we can discuss this together."

She waved a hand in front of her. "No, don't. Please. It wasn't me. I'm not the one going around killing women. I swear."

I pocketed my phone. "I'm going to need proof, Alli."

"I'll ... Look, come in, all right? But please, keep it down. I don't want to have this conversation in front of my mother. She's asleep, and I'd like to keep it that way."

"Fine. I'll come in. I'll listen. I can't promise anything beyond that."

She nodded, and I followed her downstairs, my hand hovering over the gun tucked beneath my shirt. We sat on the sectional sofa, and as soon as she plopped down and covered her legs with an afghan, the tears started flowing.

She could cry all she wanted.

It wouldn't save her now.

"Seems like such a long time ago," she began. "Almost like another lifetime."

"High school?"

She nodded.

"You're what, twenty-seven?" I asked. "Ten years isn't that long."

"You say that because you're older."

Gee, thanks.

"I say that because it's true, and you're stalling. Why?"

"Talking about the person I was when I was younger isn't easy."

"Three women are dead. Something happened in high school, something you *knew about* the first time I was here, and yet you said nothing. Don't waste my time trying to elicit sympathy."

"I didn't say anything because I didn't think our high school shenanigans had anything to do with Pippa's and Greer's murders. People do dumb stuff all the time when they're teens. Most people don't go around killing anyone over it."

"I suppose it all depends. What dumb stuff did you do?"

She pressed her hands together and went silent.

I waited.

I'd wait as long as it took, even if it took all night.

This time, I was leaving with answers.

"Pippa, Greer, Naomi, and I were all on the varsity basketball team together."

"Along with who else?"

"A lot of other girls. There were fourteen of us on the team."

"I want a list of all your teammates."

She shrugged. "Okay. I'll write them down before you leave."

Who said anything about leaving?

"Of the fourteen, which other girls did the four of you pal around with in school?"

"Most of them, but six of us were, you know, in our own clique, I guess."

"The female jocks who ran the school, you mean."

"Yeah, guess so."

"What are the names of the other two girls in the friend group?"

"Dana Kellogg and Rebecca Miller."

"Any idea where they live now?"

"No idea. I haven't spoken to those two since high school."

"Why are your old classmates dying, Alli?"

"I'm not one-hundred-percent sure."

"But you have an idea."

Another long pause.

"Some kids at school thought we were bullies."

"Were you?"

"I mean, we could be a bit on the, umm—"

"Were you bullies, or weren't you?" I asked. "It's not a hard question. Just tell the truth."

"We were. Sometimes. Not all the time."

"What kind of things did you do?"

"Stupid stuff like link our arms together in the hallway between classes and ram a few dorks into the school lockers, or we'd stand outside of the snack shack and take candy bars from some of our classmates when they came out."

It was bad, but I didn't believe she'd gotten to the worst of it yet.

"What else?"

"If Greer didn't like someone, she'd do things like stick a chewed-up piece of gum in their hair."

"Was she the ringleader of your clique?"

"Yep."

"Was it her idea to pick on some of the other girls?"

"Most of the time."

"How did you feel about it?"

"Better than I should have. I'm not that person anymore. I look back, and I'm ashamed of it."

"What about Pippa?" I asked. "How did she feel?"

"Pippa always felt bad. She'd try to talk Greer out of some of the crazy stuff she wanted to do."

"Feeling bad isn't the same as stopping it."

Alli nodded. "I guess not. We should have listened to Pippa, and I should have agreed with her. Maybe if I had, things would be different."

If by *different* she meant three women wouldn't be dead, there was a good chance she was right.

"To bully another person in any way is horrible, but why do I get the feeling there was something worse—a lot worse?"

"Yeah ... so, there were these sisters who transferred to our school when I was in my junior year. One of them, Cassie Duran, started flirting with the guy Greer was dating. It wasn't long before he dumped Greer and began dating Cassie. Greer was so upset she started a rumor."

"What was the rumor?"

"Greer told everyone Cassie had chlamydia. Everyone believed it too. I'm talking the entire school. And since our school was small enough that everyone knew each other, it took less than a day or two for it to get around."

It was an awful thing for Greer to have done.

"Did Cassie know Greer started the rumor?" I asked.

"Greer told her right to her face, and Cassie slapped her, which made Greer even angrier."

"What did she do?"

"She gave her a nickname which made things even worse."

"What was the nickname?"

"Assie Cassie. All the boys believed she had an STD, and all the girls thought she was ... well, a name I'd rather not say."

"I'm guessing after that no guys would date Cassie, and no girls wanted to be friends with her. Right?"

Alli bowed her head and nodded.

"I don't know what I find more pathetic," I said. "The fact a group of girls got their rocks off by bullying other, less popular girls. Or the fact none of you had the backbone to stand up for a girl who'd done nothing more than like a guy who liked her back."

"I'm not proud of it."

"Do you have a picture of Cassie Duran?"

"Why would I?"

"Don't you own a high school yearbook?"

She crossed the room, walked over to a cabinet, and opened it, pulling things out until she found what she wanted. Among those things was an antique book. It cracked open, and I noticed the pages were filled with symbols I didn't recognize.

"Interesting book," I said.

Alli turned, staring at the book I was looking at. "Oh, yeah. It's my boyfriend's. Looks like ancient Egyptian to me." She turned back to the cabinet, pulling out a yearbook moments later. "I'm not sure Cassie will be in here. She didn't live in the area long. After all the stuff went down at school, they moved away."

Alli flipped to the index section of the yearbook, using her finger to scan through the names on the page. "Found it. There's just one photo, the one from picture day."

Alli turned the book toward me and tapped on Cassie's photo. I leaned in, studying every inch of it, disappointed when nothing about her was recognizable. Cassie looked kind, like a person anyone would want to befriend at school.

I took out my phone and snapped Cassie's photo. "And her sister?"

"Keri Duran … she was one year younger, I think."

Alli flipped back to the previous year and scrolled through the names. "Here she is, page 65."

Keri didn't look familiar either.

"I'll take that list now, and while you're at it, go through your yearbooks and write down any women you remember bullying in any way."

Alli groaned. "It's after midnight. Can't it wait until tomorrow?"

"It can't. I'll stay until you're done."

And I did, sitting across from Alli, watching her wince as she recognized the faces of the girls she'd abused in one form or another. It looked painful, but maybe pain was what she needed right now, a harsh atonement of past sins.

Two hours later, she handed me the final list and yawned. "I'm going to bed. You can see yourself out."

"You know she's coming for you, right? Whoever she is."

"There's a police officer sitting outside. Sometimes two. I also have a security system. She's not getting in here."

Where there was a will, there was almost always a way.

I folded the piece of paper she'd given me and said, "I'll need to share this information with Detective Foley. All of it. Everything you've told me tonight. Just thought you should know."

She sighed. "Figures. Do you think it's possible the killer is Cassie Duran?"

I slung my handbag over my shoulder. "What I think is this: I hope you've learned something through all this and raise Cooper to be a better person than you were. And Alli, if someone *is* picking off girls from your little school posse, don't think one or two police officers and a security system will stop her. You'd better watch your back."

44

woke at dawn and gave Foley a call.

He answered the phone with a gruff, "What time is it?"

"It's early. Five thirty or so."

"Why are you calling me, then?"

"I have information."

"You always have information. I'm starting to think it was a mistake to give you my cell phone number."

Too late now.

"Do you want me to tell you what I've found out or not?" I said.

"I'm awake now. What's up?"

"I saw Alli Kane last night, and I'm getting ready to text you a couple of photos."

"Photos of what?"

"A woman named Cassie Duran, and her sister, Keri Duran. They attended high school with Alli, Naomi, Pippa, and Greer."

"Yes … we know."

He knew.

What else did he know?

"Did you also know those women bullied Cassie and several other girls back then?"

His silence was my answer.

He didn't know.

Two points for Team Germaine.

Now for my three-point play.

"Back in high school, Greer spread a rumor about Cassie," I said.

He scoffed. "A rumor so bad she decided to kill Greer and a couple other classmates more than a decade later?"

I told him what Alli had told me.

His response?

"*Oh.*"

"Alli said there were six girls in the bully brigade. When I went to see Wolfe, she made a comment about a hexagon, and then, as you know, she asked Blackwell to relay the message to me about the wolf seeing shapes and shadows. It's a clue. Six sides to a hexagon. Six teenage bullies. Three dead. Three more to go."

When he failed to respond, I said, "Are you there?"

"Yeah, I'm here. Don't know what to think about your hexagon theory."

"If you met Wolfe and got to know what she's like, you'd understand."

"Maybe so."

"I won't keep you," I said. "Just wanted you to know what I know. I'll also send you a list of all the girls on the basketball team, a list of any girls Alli remembered bullying in school, and the names of the other two teenage bullies."

He laughed and said, "Why don't you just send over the name of the killer while you're at it?"

It was the one thing I couldn't do—not yet.

Even though his comment was a sarcastic one, he was impressed, I could hear it in his tone of voice.

"I'm going to look into the Duran sisters today," I said.

"I'll see what I can find on my end too ... *after* I get another hour of sleep. Goodbye, Miss Germaine."

45

I t's a double espresso kind of day, is it?"

Silas shot me a wink and handed me the largest cup of dirty chai the café offered.

"Thanks. I didn't get much sleep last night," I said. "Scratch that. I didn't get any."

I zipped my jacket up all the way, and we walked across the street to Moonstone Beach to stroll along the wooden boardwalk which ran alongside the ocean. The air smelled saltier than usual today, the overcast sky offering a cheerless sense of gloom, mirroring the blasé feeling stirring inside me.

Silas stared at me for a moment and then gave me a slight nudge. "Come on, talk to me. What's up?"

"I don't get it," I said. "Why is this case so much harder to figure out than the others? Why don't I know who she is yet? I've gone over and over everyone I've interviewed. All of them have the potential to be our killer, but none of them seem to be the right one."

"You've always found the person you're after, Gigi. You will this time too."

He took a seat on one of several wooden benches peppered along the boardwalk. This one had seen better days, having been carved with a variety of different initials over time. I sat beside Silas, and we sipped our drinks, staring out at an ocean that seemed even more discontented than I was today.

"I have to find her, Silas. Her kills are getting closer together, and the fact she's keeping tabs on *my* family is maddening."

"Hey, speaking of family, I have something that will cheer you up."

"Yeah?"

"I processed the wine from the bottle left at your sister's house. And guess what? It *wasn't* poisoned."

It. Wasn't. Poisoned.

"So, she, what … is taunting me for the fun of it?"

"Looks like it."

I balled my hand into a fist, resisting the urge to slam it into the bench. I was tired of her games, tired of Wolfe's games. Just … tired.

"I have an idea," Silas said. "I was just thinking about when you became a detective for the department. The first few homicide cases you had, you struggled to solve. Remember?"

I'd almost forgotten my rookie detective years, a time when I was trying so hard to live up to my father's legacy it overshadowed everything else.

"I remember. I came to you, and we talked those cases through. Talking to you calmed me, helped shift my focus."

"I get you're a hot-shot private eye now with years of detective experience under your belt. I was just thinkin' how sometimes going back to the basics helps to see things in a different way. So lay it on me. Let's hear about all these women you're investigating."

"What would you like to know?"

"Tell me something odd about them, something you didn't put in your notes."

It was worth a try.

"For starters, there's Laney St. James," I said.

"The actress?"

"Yeah."

"Love her. She was amazing in *The Killing Hour*."

"The movie where she played a serial killer?"

He nodded. "It's the best film she's ever done, hands down. I watched the interview she did on *The Tonight Show* a couple of years back. You know, before she landed in rehab. In the interview she said it was the most favorite character she'd ever played."

I didn't doubt it—the more eccentric the better.

"Okay, so something strange about Laney. When I saw her last, she made a cocktail while I was there. She opened her fridge and pulled out this jar of specialty olives, and I noticed she had an entire shelf devoted to cosmetics—all different types of makeup. Who knew people kept stuff like that in a refrigerator?"

Silas shook his head, laughing. "Classic Laney. Who's next?"

"Alli Kane. She went to high school with all three of the victims. She claims they were bullies back then, something she didn't admit until I forced it out of her. Last night, while I was at her house, she opened a cabinet, looking for her old yearbooks. As she was taking books out, she removed a small antique book with leather binding. It fell open, and I noticed the entire book was filled with symbols."

"What kind of symbols?"

"Masonic or Egyptian, I think. I asked her about it, and she said the book belonged to her boyfriend." I went through a mental list of everyone else. "There's also Samantha Armstrong, the daughter of Pippa's boyfriend, Trevor. She had connections to Pippa and Greer, but none to Naomi, as far as I know."

"What's her story?"

"She didn't like the idea her father was dating someone half his age."

"Did you meet her?"

"Once. I went into her father's café, and she made me a drink. Every single one of her manicured fingernails was perfect except one. It looked like it had been ripped off, and the same finger had a vertical inch-long cut. I asked her about it. She said she'd slammed it into the register by accident."

Silas set his cup down and leaned back, lacing his fingers together behind his head. "This is fun. Are you having fun?"

"You know what? I'm not feeling as overwhelmed as I was a few minutes ago … so, yes. Thanks for suggesting we do this. It's helping me clear my head."

"Good. Let's keep going. Tell me about Wolfe."

"She's sharp and always seems to be one step ahead of me. I'm sure she knows who's committing these murders and why. Even though she won't reveal who the killer is, something tells me she wants me catch them, just like my father caught her."

"Maybe she knows she would have continued killing and prison was the best place for her."

"She respected my father. I can tell when I talk to her. I remind her of him. I can see it in the way she looks at me, and she mentioned it even."

"That's not creepy at all."

I laughed so hard I almost coughed up the mouthful of chai I'd just taken. "Fun fact. Donna Reagan is the only woman to ever interview Wolfe. She lives on a houseboat in Monterey. She had an entire shelf of miniature clocks—a piano, an owl, a teapot, a cat. Oh, and then there's Pippa's house cleaner, Adriana Simpson. She's obsessed with reading old issues of *The Enquirer*."

"I know her. She owns Squeaky Clean Maids, right?"

"Along with her sister, yeah."

"Her sister cleaned my house a few times. I was thrilled

when they started up because they're one of the only house cleaning services in town."

"Sounds like you're not using them anymore."

"I'm not. Last time her sister was at my house, she did a crappy job. I walked in from work, and she was sitting on my sofa, talking on her cell phone, even though half the place still wasn't clean."

"I wonder if Adriana did any housekeeping for Alli Kane. Given the size of Alli's house, I wouldn't doubt it."

"Wouldn't hurt to ask."

Silas finished the rest of his drink and glanced at his phone. "I better head in to work soon."

I slumped down, closed my eyes, and rested my head on the bench, listening to the sound of the waves hitting the shoreline. "You go ahead if you need to, Silas. I'm going to sit here for a few more minutes."

Silas leaned his head back too. "I can hang back a little longer."

As I rested my eyes, I flashed back to each visit I'd had with the women, allowing my mind to wander wherever it wanted to go, see what it wanted to see. I'd been so caught up in my impatience to solve the case, I'd lost my focus.

It was what the killer wanted.

It was what she'd always wanted.

Acute details began to emerge, things I'd seen but thought didn't matter at the time. And Wolfe's words repeating over and over in my mind ...

You can't even see what's right in front of your face.
You can't even see what's right in front of your face.
You can't even see what's right in front of your face.

She was right.

I hadn't seen it.

But in that moment, I did.

One specific detail hit me so hard my eyes burst open, and I grabbed my throat, struggling to suck in even the smallest breath.

Silas wrapped his hands around my arms. "What is it? Are you okay?"

I wasn't okay, but soon, I would be.

I turned to Silas and said, "I know who she is!"

46

*W*ell, who is she?" Silas pressed. "Don't leave me hanging. You gonna tell me which of the lucky ladies is about to have an unlucky day?"

"Can you keep it under wraps for a bit if I do?"

"As far as I'm concerned, we're not here right now, and you never told me a thing."

I leaned in close, whispering the name, and telling him how I knew it was her.

"Wow," he said. "Far out. You're going after her, aren't you?"

"I am."

"I'm not saying you should call Foley or Blackwood first, but I don't like the idea of you doing this alone."

"I won't."

"Are you just saying that to ease my mind?"

I shook my head.

"Want me to come with you?" he suggested.

"You head into work. I'll take Simone. She'd love to go."

My phone vibrated.

It was Hunter, no doubt, calling to follow up on what she'd uncovered about the Duran sisters.

I sent it to voicemail and turned toward Silas. "Here's what I'd like you to do. Wait forty-five minutes, long enough for me to make a call, grab Simone, and head to where I'm going. I'll call you. We'll stay on the phone for a minute. That way if anyone at the department questions whether you knew beforehand, you'll have my phone call to prove you called the department right after you talked to me."

"What do you want me to say?"

"First, I want you to call Foley, not Blackwell. Here's what I want you to tell him ..."

47

I ended a brief, yet enlightening call with Hunter and jerked the car to a stop in front of my brother's place. Simone was waiting at the curb, dressed in an oversized AC/DC "Highway to Hell" T-shirt, black jeans, and blood red Dr. Martens boots. The woman meant business, and I had to admit, I was feeling a little "Highway to Hell" myself.

She opened the passenger-side door and slid on in.

"You up for this?" I asked.

"Are you kidding? This is the most excited I've been in a long time. Is Hunter coming too?"

I shook my head. "She's more comfortable hanging back."

As we drove, we talked strategy. I'd go in first. Simone would wait nearby—close enough to hear me if I called out to her, but far enough away not to spook the suspect. Who was I kidding? The woman was no suspect. *She* was a cold-blooded murderer.

I pulled the car to a stop and gripped the steering wheel, my heart thumping so fast inside my chest I was starting to rethink the morning jolt of caffeine I'd had.

"Hey," Simone said. "You sure you want to stick to this plan? Because I don't mind coming in with you. We have no idea what's going to happen when you confront her."

"You're right. We don't. But when she decided to play games with my family—"

"*Our* family, Gigi."

She was right.

Simone was family now.

"I'm sorry," I said. "I didn't mean it like—"

"Hey, don't apologize. All I'm trying to say is, where family is concerned, we're in this together from now on."

I nodded, opened the door, and stepped out, facing forward, my eye on the prize. Time to see if our resident murderer was at home. "Ready?"

"Yep. Let's go."

I reached beneath my shirt, palming the gun at my waist, as I inched toward my most important stop of the day. Reaching the harbor, I took my time stepping onto the houseboat. It didn't matter. The moment my foot touched the upper deck was like a clarion call, and I heard shuffling, movement below.

I jerked around, waving Simone into position, a gesture we'd discussed earlier to indicate the suspect was at home. Step after step, I lowered myself into the cabin below, coming face-to-face with a grinning Donna Reagan, clad in nothing but a bikini. In her hand was a gun—a gun aimed at my chest.

"Took you long enough," she said.

"Donna Reagan? Or should I say Keri Duran? Which do you prefer?"

"Keri's been gone a long time. I'm Donna now. Have been for years."

"A little facial work, weight loss, dyed hair … even your eyes are different than they used to be."

"Colored contacts. Put the gun down."

"You first."

"Why should I? You're the one who's trespassing. You and your one-woman operation. You're so bent on catching me yourself you couldn't even call the police to back you up, could you? You had to take me on alone to prove you could do it. Don't get me wrong. I admire you for it. Better a woman than a man. Still, I liked you. Bad choice on your part."

We'll see.

"You plan on shooting me?"

She cocked her head to the side. "I have no choice. Do I?"

"Looks like I won't be interviewing for your magazine."

"Suppose not."

"Why didn't you poison the bottle of wine you gave to my sister?" I asked.

"The wine was never meant for her, and I wouldn't have killed her, or you, by the way, if you would have left me alone. That bottle of wine was meant to distract you, and it did. It allowed me to go about my business without you interfering."

"If I hadn't interfered, would you have stopped after you killed all six women on your hit list?"

"Six. Where did you come up with that number?"

"Wolfe."

"You're lying. She wouldn't give me away."

"She would. You think she cares about you. She doesn't."

"You don't know what you're talking about."

"How many more women are you planning on killing?"

"I might stop at six. I might not. I like how it feels, taking someone else's life. In their final moments, when they look up and realize it's me, it's a rush. Never felt anything like it."

I thought about the conversation I'd had with Hunter right before I picked up Simone. "Your sister, Cassie. She killed herself."

Her lip quivered, the uncomfortable shift in the conversation causing her to squirm in her seat.

"She overdosed on pills in college. My family choose to believe it was an accident. It wasn't. She never got past what happened in high school."

"You waited a long time to avenge her."

"I wasn't always the person I am now. Back then, when we were in school, I was weak. I did nothing to stand up for her. Not a single thing. After she died, the guilt consumed me, until the day I was reaching for a can of soup at the grocery store, and guess who I ran into?"

"Pippa?"

She nodded. "I don't know how, but she recognized me. She asked how Cassie was doing. When I told her, she was full of apologies. She was sorry she didn't stand up for her. Sorry she did nothing to stop her sister or squash the rumor. Sorry Cassie was dead. I realized all these years I'd felt sorry too, and then it hit me. Sorry isn't how I needed to feel. I needed to feel angry."

"Feeling angry is one thing. Killing over it is another."

She grunted a laugh. "You should have seen how awkward Pippa was when she learned about my sister. She stood there, stumbling over her words, trying to seem sympathetic about a former classmate she never cared about. It disgusted me."

"How did the exchange at the grocery store end?"

"With Pippa trying to make amends for something she couldn't."

The gun in her hand was wavering. I needed to keep her talking, positioning myself for the perfect time to strike.

"What amends did Pippa try to make?" I asked.

"She invited me to her place. Guess she thought we could be friends. I mean, I always knew she was naïve, but she was even more ignorant than I thought."

"Did you go?"

She nodded. "There I was, staring out at the sunset from the deck of her ridiculous mansion. It was beautiful, but all I could think about was how many sunsets my sister had missed over the years. As Pippa stood next to me, talking about her perfect life, something inside me snapped. It was like the lid I'd used to bottle everything inside—all the anger, hurt, rage—burst open."

"You've changed your hair over the last several weeks. Is it because Pippa's housekeeper caught the two of you arguing in the driveway?"

"Yep, do you like it?"

"What were you arguing about?"

"Pippa had just donated a bunch of money to a new museum—you know the one they're building downtown in Los Angeles."

"What about it?"

"Her donation was large enough for her name to be put on a plaque along with a bunch of other rich bastards. She wanted to put my sister's name on the plaque instead of hers."

"Seems like a nice gesture."

"A nice gesture? You can't *buy* forgiveness."

I thought about the argument Donovan Grant had witnessed between Pippa and Greer the night of the dinner party. Perhaps I'd never know what had been said, but I'd narrowed it down to one of two things. Either Pippa had come clean about her relationship with Trevor Armstrong or she'd told Greer about the friendship she was trying to ignite with their old classmate. The last thing Greer would have wanted was the two of them becoming friends.

"What made you take a job at *Serial Crime Magazine*?" I asked.

"I had a degree in journalism, and homicides have always fascinated me. When I first started at the magazine, they gave me a list of names of all the serial killers they'd never been able to get an interview with over the years. If I managed to get an interview with one of them, they promised to give me a significant raise and a higher position. Wolfe was at the top of my list. I've always admired her."

"After years of refusing interviews, why did Wolfe pick you?"

"In my first letter to her, I was honest. I told her my sister's story and said I understood why she'd killed all those women."

"How often did the two of you write to each other?"

"A few times, enough to give her an idea I wasn't just after an interview."

"I have a list of everyone who wrote to her in the last year. It shows you wrote her once."

"Under the name Donna Reagan, yes."

Sneaky.

"A few parts of the conversation between the two of you never made it into the article."

"Let's just say she gave me some sage advice, and I took it. The woman is brilliant, unlike anyone I've ever met."

"You idolize her."

"Don't you?"

"I don't."

She squinted at me. "I have a question. How did you know it was me?"

"Two things gave you away, the first being the name of your boat, *Static Flow*. Rearrange the letters and you get Attics Wolf. Close enough."

"You like it? I just had it painted a month ago."

A month ago, right around the time her article was published, no doubt.

"And the second?" she asked.

"The clocks on your shelf. The times are all different. At first, I assumed you did what a lot of people do—set each clock to reflect the time in a different part of the world. You said you were well-traveled. It made sense, until it didn't. Each clock is set to the exact time of death of your three victims." I tipped my head toward the cat clock. "Except the time on this one."

"The cat clock belonged to my sister. It's set to the time she overdosed."

"I know you won't, but you should turn yourself in. This doesn't need to end in a shootout."

"I won't rot away in some prison."

"How will you justify killing me? I don't fit your MO."

"You sure?"

"How could I?"

"Are you saying you never bullied anyone your entire life? You never broke the law in the line of duty? Never hurt someone who didn't deserve it? I'm guessing you have. You look at me, and all you see is a clone of Wolfe, except I don't murder according to some stupid code. I'll kill you right now."

She squeezed the trigger, the gunshot echoing throughout the cabin, as I fired back. In a foggy haze, I felt myself falling backward, and Simone hovering over me, saying, "Stay, stay with me, Gigi."

48

An hour later, I sat on the houseboat's upper deck and stripped off my bulletproof vest, assessing the damage to my shoulder. The impact of the bullet was going to leave a bruise—a big nasty-looking one—and that was okay.

Foley walked up and sat next to me, the look on his face indicating he had half a mind to wring my neck. "You shoot the suspect in almost the same spot she shoots you, and then Simone rushes in behind you and punches her in the face."

Good for Simone.

"I could have killed her," I said. "I didn't."

"What am I supposed to do with the two of you?"

"Thank us?"

"Thank you? For what?"

"I solved your murder."

"We were onto her, just so you know."

"Yeah, well, I guess I was *onto her* first."

"You never let up with the sarcasm, do you?"

"Do you?"

He shook his head, laughing.

I pulled my cell phone out of my pocket and pressed play, allowing Foley to listen in on the first thirty seconds of the handy-dandy recording I'd made.

"It's a full confession," I said, stating the obvious.

"I suppose the next thing you're going to do is ask for an exchange —no charges filed against you and your cohort, and you'll give me the recording."

"Smart guy."

"And if I don't agree?"

"I don't know," I said. "Cell phones get damaged all the time. Would be a shame if something happened to mine and the recording was lost."

He tugged at his chin, mulling over the proposition. "Okay, fine."

His response came faster than I'd expected. Then again, he hadn't taken his eyes off my cell phone since I played the recording.

"Is it fine though?" I asked.

"Why wouldn't it be?"

"Blackwell's wanted to nail me to the wall since the day we met."

"Let me handle him."

No one *handled* Blackwell.

"Good luck," I said.

"I don't need luck. I need logic."

As if Blackwell's ears were ringing, he emerged from the lower level of the houseboat, making a beeline for the two of us.

"Aren't you two chummy," he began.

It was my cue to leave.

I stood. "I'll drop by the department when I get back into town and give my statement."

"You will not. You're not going anywhere, Germaine."

Simone walked over and stood beside me, crossing her arms in front of her and staring Blackwell down without uttering a single word.

"Like I said, I'll drop by the department, but I *am* leaving." I turned toward Simone. "You ready to go?"

"Yep."

We walked away, Blackwell shouting expletives in the distance as Foley tried and failed at calming him down.

49

I walked the familiar path through the cemetery, stopping first to visit my daughter's grave before heading over to see my father. When I reached his headstone, I noticed I wasn't the only one who'd been there in recent days. There was a beautiful bouquet of lilies, which I assumed had been left by my mother, who still stopped by almost every week.

I sat on the grass and did what I always did when I visited. I talked to him like he was there with me, listening to my every word.

Hey, Dad …
I just solved my first case as a private investigator.
You'd be proud of me.
I think you would be anyway.
Just when I think I know everything about you, I learn something new.

Makes me wish you'd left a journal behind.

I met someone you arrested a long time ago, but I won't waste our time together talking about her.

Everyone's good.

Mom's still doing Pilates a few times a week, Harvey's pretending to enjoy retirement, and Paul and Simone are planning their wedding. Wish you could have met Simone. You'd like her.

Let's see ... who else haven't I mentioned?

Nathan's still traveling the world, and Phoebe and Lark are doing good. Lark's getting so big. And smart! She's like a tiny adult.

As for me, I feel happier than I have in a long time.

Working for myself has its perks.

Everything's going great with Giovanni too.

Well ... I'm meeting up with Simone and Hunter in a bit, so I guess I should get going. Give Fallon a big kiss for me, would you?

I kissed my hand and touched it to his headstone, noticing what appeared to be a small card sticking out of the lily bouquet. I reached for it, staring for a moment at the tiny, sealed envelope.

How odd.

The flowers Mom left never came with a card.

I broke the seal on the envelope and pulled out the card, goosebumps spreading up my arm as I read its contents.

Well done, Germaine.
Until next time, Atticus Wolfe

She had it all wrong.

There wouldn't be a next time.

50

Simone walked into the room with a perplexed look on her face. She eyed Hunter and then me and said, "So, umm, who's the dude standing outside?"

I leaned over, staring out the window at Peppe. "Ahh ... let's call him security for now."

"Security, eh? Why does security look like Al Capone?"

Hunter snorted a laugh.

"Maybe they're related," I said. "You should ask him."

Simone crossed her arms and joined in on Hunter's laughter. "Maybe I will."

I spread my arms wide and spun around. "Well, what do you think? Do you like it?"

Simone looked around the office space and smiled. "It's fantastic. This will be perfect for us."

"What about you, Hunter?"

"I love it!"

"I know it's a studio and we don't have individual offices, but—"

"We don't need our own offices," Hunter said. "We're a team."

"I agree," Simone added.

"Good. As for what I want to do with this place, I'm thinking we keep the urban loft vibe going but make a few upgrades."

"Like what?" Simone asked.

"We'll leave the exposed brick, paint the overhead pipes black, rip up the carpet, and put an acrylic sealer over the concrete slab. Oh, and get that old-fashioned fireplace going again."

"A *few* upgrades, huh?" Hunter said. "Sounds more like an entire revamp."

"I love the bones in this old place," Simone said. "It has a good feel to it."

I agreed.

When I was through with it, the space would be warm and welcoming, a place where people could kick up their feet and stay a while.

A *little* while.

I pointed to the center of the room. "We can line our desks up in a U shape over there, and then put a wood table and chairs on one side of the room and sectional sofa on the other. When new clients come in, I want them to feel comfortable and safe, like they're with a trusted family member."

"I can't wait to get started," Hunter said. "I've already created some ads online to bring in business. There's still one thing left to do though."

"What's that?" I asked.

"We need a name. What are we going to call ourselves?"

Simone snapped her fingers and said, "How about Badass Beauties Detective Agency, or Clued-in Detective Agency, Sassy Sherlocks, or Prowl Patrol Detective Agency?"

Hunter cupped a hand over her mouth, giggling. "*Prowl Patrol?*"

"Oh, come on," Simone said. "It's not that bad. If you think you can do better, go for it."

"Challenge accepted," Hunter said. "Let's see … I'm thinking something like Women's Protective Bureau, or Private Eye Services."

Standing with them now, I appreciated how different they were in personality. Simone the carefree, fun-loving type, a sharp contrast to Hunter's take-life-serious approach. And then there was me, part loose cannon, part adult in training, and completely devoted to solving each case that came our way.

"Thank you for your suggestions," I said. "I like them both. Here's what I'm thinking … Case Closed Detective Agency."

"Ooh, I like it," Simone said.

"Me too."

And there we had it.

Case Closed Detective Agency, three fierce women ready to take on their next case.

…

Thank you for reading Little White Lies, book four in the *USA Today* bestselling Georgiana Germaine mystery series.

I hope you enjoyed getting to know the characters in this story as much as I have enjoyed writing them for you. This is a continuing series with more books coming before and after the one you just read. You can find the series order (as of the date of this printing) in the "Books by Cheryl Bradshaw" section below.

In Little Tangled Webs, book five in the series, eighteen-year-old Harper Ellis has spent the last three years searching for her aunt's killer, looking for clues, asking questions, gathering every tidbit she can find to explain the unexplainable. She's talked to anyone who would listen, trying to make them to see they're all wrong, and she is right.

Aunt Frida's death *wasn't* an accident. Aunt Frida was murdered. Of this, Harper is certain. Tonight, Harper plans prove her theory, and she's prepared to risk her own life to do it.

Want a sneak peek? Here's an exclusive look at chapter one …

LITTLE TANGLED WEBS

GEORGIANA GERMAINE SERIES BOOK 5

1

Harper Ellis leaned back on her pillow, staring at the framed photo sitting atop her dresser. In the picture, Harper and her Aunt Frida were arm in arm, smiling, the joyous memory now frozen in time. It had been three years since Aunt Frida had died. Three years since her death had been ruled an accident. Three years … and everyone had moved on.

Everyone except Harper.

Harper had spent those years digging, looking for clues, asking questions, gathering every tidbit she could find to explain the unexplainable. She talked to anyone who would listen, trying to make them to see they were wrong, and she was right.

Aunt Frida's death *wasn't* an accident.

She'd been murdered.

Of this, Harper was certain.

At first, most of Aunt Frida's friends and family indulged Harper's theories to a degree. They assumed she was grieving as they were. But as time passed, and Harper refused to let her suspicions go, they grew tired of hearing them. Soon after, her uncle asked her not to speak of her aunt's death again—not to him or anyone else—and suggested she put her ludicrous theories to rest.

Harper pulled the photo frame off the dresser and clutched it in her hands, reminiscing about the day the picture was taken. It was Harper's fifteenth birthday. Friends and family had gathered at the park to celebrate. They had a barbecue and took pictures under a gazebo her mother had decorated with balloons and twinkle lights.

It was one of the happiest days of Harper's life.

It was also the last time she saw her Aunt Frida alive.

A soft rapping sound on the bedroom door snapped Harper back into the present moment. She returned the photo frame to its usual spot and said, "Come in."

Her mother poked her head inside.

"Have you decided what you're wearing to the wedding tomorrow?" she asked.

"It's okay to dress in all black, right?"

Her mother wasn't amused. "Not funny, Harper."

"I'm kidding, Mom."

"I know you are, honey. What are you up to tonight?"

"The usual. Hanging out with friends."

"Don't stay out too late. We need to leave here at nine thirty to get to the beach before the ceremony begins."

"I'll be ready, Mom."

Her mother smiled and closed the door.

It was a rare occasion when Harper lied to her mother. But revealing her actual plans for the evening was out of the question. Tonight, she was testing her latest theory, and this time, she was ninety percent sure she had it right. Step one in the confirmation process required her to leave a note beneath the windshield of a certain person's vehicle. A note that said:

Meet me at Shamel Park, at the gazebo. Tonight. Eight o'clock. Don't show, and I'll tell everyone what really happened to Frida.

A few months earlier, Harper had stumbled upon an important clue in her quest to prove Frida's death wasn't an accident. Now it was time to see if she was right. If she was, she needed to get him to say something to incriminate himself.

Given the fact no one had believed her up to this point, Harper knew she'd need help if she was to bring Frida's killer to justice. Over the last three months, she'd been planning and saving, preparing for today.

Soon everyone would know the truth.

Soon, Aunt Frida's killer would pay.

Unsure of how her suspect would take the news when he was confronted, Harper invested in a little protection. She pulled open her dresser drawer, riffling through it until she found the pocketknife she'd purchased. She stuck it into her purse and glanced at the mirror, pulling her blond, wavy hair back into a loose ponytail. She dabbed a bit of clear gloss over her lips and reached for her car keys.

It was seven thirty-five.

Go time.

Harper gave her mother a quick wave goodbye and headed out the door. She walked to the car and got inside, gripping the steering wheel as she inhaled a lungful of air. Her heart was beating fast—too fast. But there wasn't much she could do about that.

On the car ride over, she rehearsed what she wanted to say in her mind. The words she would use needed to be precise. They needed to provoke him, to make him talk, to prove whether he was the man she was after.

Harper pulled to a stop at the park's entrance and exited the car. Tonight seemed warmer than usual. A quiet stillness filled the air, and there wasn't much light, just a sliver of a moon peeking out from behind the clouds.

She scanned the area, didn't see anyone. Perhaps he wasn't here yet. She checked the time. Five minutes to spare, right on schedule.

Harper walked the grassy path to the gazebo and waited.

Five minutes passed.

Then ten.

Then twenty.

At half past eight, it was obvious he wasn't coming. She strolled back to the car, disappointed the night hadn't gone as planned. She'd chosen to meet at the gazebo because of its significance.

No matter.

A new plan was forming.

If he didn't want to come to her, she'd go to him.

Harper pulled the driver's-side door open, jolting backward when a gray cat darted out from beneath a picnic table next to the gazebo. The cat turned toward her, narrowing his eyes as if she was trespassing on his domain.

Crazy cat.

You scared the bejesus out of me.

She huffed a slight laugh and got into the car. Slipping her seatbelt over her waist, she put the key into the ignition. A hand reached out from behind, then two, fingers, thick and strong, as they wrapped around her neck. Squeezing.

Harper tried to scream and couldn't.

She tried reaching for the pocketknife, but the tight grip of the seatbelt wouldn't allow it.

She curled her fingers around his, desperate to peel them off her, but his grip was firm, unmoving. The man leaned forward, his hot breath filtering inside her ear as he uttered the last words she'd ever hear in this life. "For the record, Harper … you were right."

LITTLE WHITE LIES – AFTERWORD

In the book you've just read I covered the subject of bullying, a troubling part of society today. Bullying in any form is wrong and sadly is often dished out by individuals who are suffering from low self-esteem and a lack of self-worth themselves. For those individuals, instead of seeking help, they choose to lash out at others, pulling them down into a vicious cycle that leads to anxiety, depression, fear, stress, and even suicide.

By increasing our awareness, we can identify such bullies and stop them from harming others. We can also step in, helping victims of bullying get the assistance they need to recover from the mistreatment they've endured. We can also be there for them, letting them know they are loved, letting them know they are not alone.

If you have experienced bullying in your own life or know someone who is, here are some websites to assist in starting the journey of healing.

Here's to supporting each other. – Cheryl

Learn more about bullying by visiting the following websites online:

Stomp Out Bullying
Stop Bullying
Give us a Shout
What to do if You're Being Bullied
Anxiety and Depression Association
Suicide Prevention Hotline

About Cheryl Bradshaw

Cheryl Bradshaw is a *New York Times* and 11-time *USA Today* bestselling author writing in the genres of mystery, thriller, paranormal suspense, and romantic suspense, among others. Her novel *Stranger in Town* (Sloane Monroe series #4) was a Shamus Award finalist for Best PI Novel of the Year, and her novel *I Have a Secret* (Sloane Monroe series #3) was an eFestival of Words winner for Best Thriller.

Raised in California, most of the year she can be found exploring the tropics in Cairns, Australia, where she currently lives, or traveling the world.

Books by Cheryl Bradshaw

Sloane Monroe Series

Silent as the Grave (Prequel, Book 0)
When the body of Rebecca Barlow is found floating in the lake, private investigator Sloane Monroe takes on her very first homicide.

Black Diamond Death (Book 1)
Charlotte Halliwell has a secret. But before revealing it to her sister, she's found dead.

Murder in Mind (Book 2)
A woman is found murdered, the serial killer's trademark "S" carved into her wrist.

I Have a Secret (Book 3)
Doug Ward has been running from his past for twenty years. But after his fourth whisky of the night, he doesn't want to keep quiet, not anymore.

Stranger in Town (Book 4)
A frantic mother runs down the aisles, searching for her missing daughter. But little Olivia is already gone.

Bed of Bones (Book 5) (USA Today Bestselling Book)
Sometimes even the deepest, darkest secrets find their way to the surface.

Flirting with Danger (Book 5.5) A Sloane Monroe Short Story
A fancy hotel. A weekend getaway. For Sloane Monroe, rest has finally arrived, until the lights go out, a woman screams, and Sloane's nightmare begins.

Hush Now Baby (Book 6) (USA Today Bestselling Book)
Serena Westwood tiptoes to her baby's crib and looks inside, startled to find her newborn son is gone.

Dead of Night (Book 6.5) A Sloane Monroe Short Story
After her mother-in-law is fatally stabbed, Wren is seen fleeing with the bloody knife. Is Wren the killer, or is a dark, scandalous family secret to blame?

Gone Daddy Gone (Book 7) (USA Today Bestselling Book)
A man lurks behind Shelby in the park. Who is he? And why does he have a gun?

Smoke & Mirrors (Book 8) (USA Today Bestselling Book)
Grace Ashby wakes to the sound of a horrifying scream. She races down the hallway, finding her mother's lifeless body on the floor in a pool of blood. Her mother's boyfriend Hugh is hunched over her, but is Hugh really her mother's killer?

Sloane Monroe Stories: Deadly Sins

Deadly Sins: Sloth (Book 1)
Darryl has been shot, and a mysterious woman is sprawled out on the floor in his hallway. She's dead too. Who is she? And why

have they both been murdered?

Deadly Sins: Wrath (Book 2)
Headlights flash through Maddie's car's back windshield, someone following close behind. When her car careens into a nearby tree, the chase comes to an end. But for Maddie, the end is just the beginning.

Deadly Sins: Lust (Book 3)
Marissa Calhoun sits alone on a beach-like swimming hole nestled on Australia's foreshore. Tonight, the lagoon is hers and hers alone. Or is it?

Deadly Sins: Greed (Book 4)
It was just another day for mob boss Giovanni Luciana until he took his car for a drive.

Deadly Sins: Envy (Book 5)
A cryptic message. A missing niece. And only twenty-four hours to pay.

Sloane & Maddie, Peril Awaits
(Co-Authored with Janet Fix)

The Silent Boy (Book 1)
In the hallway of a local tavern, six-year-old Louie Alvarez waits for his mother to take him home. A scream rips through the air, followed by the sound of a gun being fired. Louie freezes, then turns, with a single thought on his mind: RUN.

The Shadow Children (Book 2)
Within the tunnels of the historic port city of Savannah, fourteen-year-old Andi Leland has her mind set on freedom—not just for

herself but for all the other teens who have come before her.

The Broken Soul (Book 3)
When the party of a lifetime becomes a party to the death, the lines become blurred. Friends become enemies. Drugs become weapons. And that's just the beginning.

Georgiana Germaine Series

Little Girl Lost (Book 1)
For the past two years, former detective Georgiana "Gigi" Germaine has been living off the grid, until today, when she hears some disturbing news that shakes her.

Little Lost Secrets (Book 2)
When bones are discovered inside the walls during a home renovation, Georgiana uncovers a secret that's linked to her father's untimely death thirty years earlier.

Little Broken Things (Book 3)
Twenty-year-old Olivia Spencer sits at her desk in her mother's bookshop, dreaming about her upcoming wedding. The store may be closed, but she's not alone, and her dream is about to become her worst nightmare.

Little White Lies (Book 4)
When a serial killer sweeps through the streets of Cambria, California, Georgiana Germaine gets swept up into a tangled web of deception and lies.

Little Tangled Webs (Book 5)
What if you knew the person you loved was murdered, but no one else believed you? Eighteen-year-old Harper Ellis knows she's right,

and she's prepared to risk her life to prove it.

Addison Lockhart Series

Grayson Manor Haunting (Book 1)
When Addison Lockhart inherits Grayson Manor after her mother's untimely death, she unlocks a secret that's been kept hidden for over fifty years.

Rosecliff Manor Haunting (Book 2)
Addison Lockhart jolts awake. The dream had seemed so real. Eleven-year-old twins Vivian and Grace were so full of life, but they couldn't be. They've been dead for over forty years.

Blackthorn Manor Haunting (Book 3)
Addison Lockhart leans over the manor's window, gasping when she feels a hand on her back. She grabs the windowsill to brace herself, but it's too late--she's already falling.

Belle Manor Haunting (Book 4)
A vehicle barrels through the stop sign, slamming into the car Addison Lockhart is inside before fleeing the scene. Who is the driver of the other car? And what secrets within the walls of Belle Manor will provide the answer?

Till Death do us Part Novella Series

Whispers of Murder (Book 1)
It was Isabelle Donnelly's wedding day, a moment in time that should have been the happiest in her life...until it ended in murder.

Echoes of Murder (Book 2)
When two women are found dead at the same wedding, medical examiner Reagan Davenport will stop at nothing to discover the identity of the killer.

Stand-Alone Novels

Eye for Revenge (USA Today Bestselling Book)
Quinn Montgomery wakes to find herself in the hospital. Her childhood best friend Evie is dead, and Evie's four-year-old son witnessed it all. Traumatized over what he saw, he hasn't spoken.

The Perfect Lie
When true-crime writer Alexandria Weston is found murdered on the last stop of her book tour, fellow writer Joss Jax steps in to investigate.

Hickory Dickory Dead (USA Today Bestselling Book)
Maisie Fezziwig wakes to a harrowing scream outside. Curious, she walks outside to investigate, and Maisie stumbles on a grisly murder that will change her life forever.

Roadkill (USA Today Bestselling Book)
Suburban housewife Juliette Granger has been living a secret life ... a life that's about to turn deadly for everyone she loves.